# THE FARADIS - BOOK EIGHT OF THE SHADOW ORDER

## MICHAEL ROBERTSON

Email: subscribers@michaelrobertson.co.uk

Edited by:

Terri King - http://terri-king.wix.com/editing
And
Pauline Nolet - http://www.paulinenolet.com

Cover Design by The Cover Collection

**The Faradis: Book Eight of The Shadow Order**

Michael Robertson
© 2018 Michael Robertson

*The Faradis: Book Eight of The Shadow Order* is a work of fiction. The characters, incidents, situations, and all dialogue are entirely a product of the author's imagination, or are used fictitiously and are not in any way representative of real people, places or things.

Any resemblance to persons living or dead is entirely coincidental.

## MAILING LIST

If you'd like to be notified of my news, discounts, and new releases, you can sign up to my spam-free mailing list at www.michaelrobertson.co.uk

# CHAPTER 1

Despite gulping several times, it did nothing to ease the lump in SA's throat. She'd just watched Reyes leave at her behest. She'd taken the choice out of her hands by busting the door's mechanism so she couldn't get back in. And what about Seb? For the first time in her life, she felt ready to settle down. Now she'd lost the lot. But she'd made the correct decision. Whatever happened, she couldn't let the third transmission get out. She couldn't put her needs above the galaxy's, and she couldn't let anyone else take her place on this suicide mission.

The room had similar features to the one Sparks had set off her flash bang in. A balcony suggested a first floor, but there were no visible doors. Not that SA could rely on that assessment. Like in the previous room, she had to assume the walls around them were capable of revealing Enigma's army from unseen entrances.

Where SA saw similarity, she also saw the differences too. The ceiling ran over this room as a large dome decorated with an intricate pattern of flowers, many of which she didn't recognise. It looked like it might have been used as a ballroom in the past. Unlike the room they'd been in previously, at present there were only three doors open: the one she'd just entered through, and two at the opposite end of the large room at least thirty metres away, where a steady stream of soldiers poured in.

SA lifted the leveller in the air. An already sore throat, she spoke anyway. "Stay there!" The large room threw her voice back at her, and she balked at the sound of it. It had been so long since she'd heard it aloud. It sounded nothing like the one in her head.

A mandulu at the head of the ever-increasing army used both its hands and pushed down on the air in front of it as it said, "Just calm down." The dumb brute must have been one of their leaders.

Fury started in SA's toes and streaked up her. It exploded from her mouth while she jabbed her finger at the creature. Her voice broke from the strain. "*Don't* you tell me to calm down." She bit the pin from the leveller and spat it away. It hit the crystal floor with a light, but very audible *ting*. "*I'm* the one calling the shots here."

The mandulu dropped its attention to the floor and stepped back a pace. It then looked up at her again and waited. The imbecile clearly had no problem with following orders. Being one of Enigma's soldiers, it obviously hadn't been employed for its initiative.

Not quite silence, but considering how many of them were in the room with more entering all the time, it was as good as. SA stood with the vast expanse of floor between them and watched the army's numbers swell. She then stepped closer to the transmitter in the middle of the room. Pyramidical in shape, at least three metres tall, and made from metal and wires, it resembled a tipi.

The constant stream of guards through the doors forced those at the front closer to SA as they elbowed and jostled for position. She waved the leveller in their direction. "I could drop this now. It'll turn this room and the transmitter to dust. It's what I've come here to do. I don't want to kill all of you with it, but your safety *isn't* my number one priority. I'm sure many of you have been brainwashed to think you're doing the right thing working for Enigma, but I wouldn't mind betting that many more are doing this work out of desperation. Whatever your reasons, this is your second chance. Pull back. Go home to your loved ones and start a new career. Again, I have no desire to hurt any of you, but *nothing* will stop me doing what I came here to do."

A slight smile twisted the dumb mandulu's face. It pulled its shoulders back as it straightened its spine. It had the confidence of a gambler holding a royal flush. It had it all worked out. "What, you'll blow yourself up too?"

A glance over both its left and right shoulder at the army surrounding it, SA saw its confidence spread through the pack. Many of them raised their weapons as if they'd just gained the advantage.

SA slipped her hand inside her top, retrieved one of the many knives in her tightly fitted harness, and threw it straight at the thing. Before the mandulu had time to move, the blade found its face and sank into it to the hilt.

The room had been quiet before, but when the mandulu fell flat on its back—the slap of it hitting the ground going off like a thunderclap—it fell quieter still.

A sharp pang turned through SA at having to kill the beast, but she didn't have time to dwell on it. If it took for her to kill one of them for the others to take her seriously, then the sacrifice was worth it. They had a minute until transmission, a minute to clear out of the room, at the most. Hopefully Reyes had gotten far enough away. And Seb ... She shook her head to banish the thought of him and blinked against the itch of tears burning her eyes. Her own feelings weren't important. They had to serve the greater good. "I have more knives." She pointed at the dead mandulu. "Anyone else want to go the way of that clown there?"

Silence.

"I didn't think so. I suggest you back out of this room now before I have to force you out!"

An instant bottleneck, the creatures turned and quietly shoved their way from the room.

"Quicker!" SA said, her voice echoing again. "You have less than one minute before I blow this place sky-high."

Then SA saw it. As the army fought to get out of there, the smaller beings were shoved back and remained in the room. A creature no taller than Sparks, it looked even smaller from how it hunched because of the weight of the cannon on its back. It had milky white eyes and dark green leathery skin. It looked like it belonged at the bottom of a well, lurking amongst mossy green rocks. A pathetic beast, it cowered when she shouted, "You!"

The creature slowly turned around, its off-white eyes wide on its small face.

"Is that some kind of plasma cannon on your back?"

A short sharp nod.

"Drop it."

A quick twist, it slipped out of the cannon, left it on the floor, and took two steps back. It stared at her as if awaiting further instruction.

"Now *go*!"

SA waited for another ten to fifteen seconds, watching the creatures disperse while she tapped her foot to spend some of her impatience. Too much longer and she'd be too late to stop the broadcast. The gap between the closest soldier and the cannon now large enough for the weapon to be isolated, she jogged to it and picked it up, her focus on the army in case they tried anything stupid.

The weight of the cannon surprised her, but it wasn't so heavy she couldn't lift it with one hand. Designed to be worn like a gauntlet, it had a sleeve, which she slid her arm into. The trigger sat at the end and she wrapped her finger around it.

Fatigue, the weight of the weapon, and apprehension about what lay ahead made SA shake while aiming the thing at the wall to her right. She needed to see what it could do. After one last check on the army, she squeezed her trigger finger.

The sound shook the walls as the cannon birthed a meteor of a blast. Unprepared for the recoil, SA flew backwards through the air, her feet lifting clean off the floor. The cannon in one hand, the pin-less leveller in the other, she didn't let go of either as she sailed in a wide arc away from the shot. She landed, her shoulder blades hitting the floor first followed by the back of her head. It drove the wind from her body and left her ears ringing.

When SA sat up, she saw how the cannon had torn through the palace. A tunnel of a hole ran through several rooms and gave her a view of the outside, the sun glistening off the stalt desert. How far did the blast go beyond the palace? It felt like she could send the next one into orbit if she wished.

The army all watched her as she got to her feet, taking great care to keep her grip tight on the leveller. "What are you looking at? Get out of here for your own sake."

While the army continued to retreat, SA pulled in deep breaths to recover from her fall and aimed the cannon at the transmitter. This time she widened her stance and planted her feet. She gripped tight enough on the leveller to not drop it, even if she did get launched again. One final deep breath, she pulled the trigger.

The thing kicked like swoink, damn near dislocating SA's shoulder and sending her sliding back several metres, the soles of her boots scraping over the ground, but she remained upright. What had once been a transmitter now existed as a pile of metal and stalt dust. The red blast had travelled through it and punched a hole in the opposite wall to the one she'd done her test shot on. It too ran all the way through to the desert beyond.

The army had stopped again. They didn't need to be as urgent, not now she'd blown up the transmitter. But she still had an armed leveller. If only she'd seen the cannon earlier, she could have scared the army off with some well-aimed blades rather than the threat of going atomic. You couldn't change your mind with a leveller. Once you'd taken the pin out, something had to get blown up.

SA looked from left to right at the damage done by the plasma cannon. She'd just opened up two more entry points. How long before more of Enigma's soldiers came at her from that way? "Now," she said to the army, "I plan on getting out of this place alive. To do that, I need to stop you lot from chasing me. Do any of you have a problem with that? Do you intend to follow me when I run?"

None of the creatures spoke. Who was she kidding? Of course they intended to follow her. Having their head turned to mist by the plasma cannon had to be better than anything Enigma would do to them if they didn't give chase.

While flicking the cannon at the soldiers to shoo them away— many of them flinching from her action—SA said, "Keep going. I want all of you out of this room, now."

She could take the grenade with her, but if she dropped it at the wrong moment, she'd be screwed. There were a lot of creatures to run away from. It wouldn't be easy to protect the leveller during the chase. Yet, if she opened fire on them with the cannon, it wouldn't drive them back; the recharge time made it ineffective for battle. Despite the damage she'd do with one shot, they'd rush her before she could get the next one off. Her advantage remained in the armed grenade. They knew what it could do—most beings in the galaxy knew what it could do. She just needed to find the best way to use it.

As she watched the last of Enigma's army move back through the doors they'd used to enter the room, SA looked at the balcony above them. She stepped back towards the door she'd used to enter the room.

Now they'd all but cleared out, some of the soldiers remained in the doorways watching her.

Another step back, SA kept her attention on them. They stayed put, although several of them gave away their intention by the way they leaned ever so slightly towards her. They were ready to charge the second she played her hand.

Now close enough to the doors, SA stood a good chance of getting away even if the army did open fire. She shouted across the large room, "If you want to survive this, you'd best run. *Now!*" She wound her arm back before launching the leveller in a wide arc at the doorway where the army waited.

For a second, SA's heart beat in her throat as she watched the leveller fly through the air. It looked like it was going to fall short, but it made it. Just. It hit the railing running around the balcony above the door with a *ting* before falling over it to the other side. Those of the army who remained all looked up at where it had landed. Not that they'd be able to see it through the cloudy stalt floor above them. While they were distracted, SA spun on her heel and sprinted away from the room.

Flat out, SA raised the cannon at the door she'd locked to prevent Reyes following her and pulled the trigger. The recoil felt like it could shatter her shoulder if she used the weapon many more times. But it did the trick, turning the door to dust.

As she ran through the hole she'd just made, SA dropped her cannon and listened to the loud thunderclap of the leveller detonating in the transmitter room.

The vibration from the explosion rattled SA's vision, and her legs nearly went beneath her, but she fought against it with wobbly steps and kept running in the direction she'd seen Reyes go. The sound of collapse ripped and snapped around her. It wouldn't be long before the entire place came crashing down.

## CHAPTER 2

The sound of the collapsing palace followed on SA's heels as a raging torrent. The bellowing wash of the shattering crystal told her it would tear her to shreds when it caught her. Despite her initial wobble, she'd now found her legs and opened up her stride. Although light-footed, the narrow and hard stalt mineral corridors still threw the sound of her steps back at her, a metronome to the cacophony of destruction racing after her.

A left turn, then a right, then a left—the corridors all looked the same. No more than eight feet wide and ten feet tall, they had no features to distinguish the flat and plain walls of one section from the flat and plain walls of another. SA had no idea where she would end up; hopefully, she hadn't already doubled back on herself. Driven by what chased her rather than a specific destination, as long as she ended up outside and remained ahead of the destruction, it didn't matter.

When SA rounded the next corner, she found the way blocked by six to eight soldiers ranging from just over five feet tall to just over eight feet. A small group, but enough of them to block her way.

The soldiers' jaws fell quicker than they could draw their weapons. SA had a more level head than them. Before the leader of the pack could do anything other than stare at her—its wide, green, reptilian eyes almost glazed with its state of shock—she threw one of her knives at it without missing a step.

The blade closed the few metres between them and struck true, straight in the centre of the brown-skinned thing's face. Much like had happened with the mandulu, it sank to the hilt and turned the beast limp. The tall creature fell back.

SA continued forward and leaped, feet first, at the falling brute. The soles of her boots slammed against the creature's wide chest, speeding up its fall as she rode it down like a skater dropping their deck into a half-pipe.

While the lizard's body fell, SA threw three more blades. Like the one aimed at the leader, all of them struck true, each one hitting a soldier. Two took knives in the face; one, in the neck.

Still at full speed, SA didn't have time to draw any more blades before an explosion of light clattered into the side of her head. Because she'd been moving so quickly, she stumbled several steps past the trio of remaining soldiers before she fell, spreading her hands out in front of her to soften her fall.

The rough stalt ground raked fire over SA's palms. When she came to a halt—the coppery taste of her own blood on the back of her tongue—she flipped onto her back and drew a knife with each stinging hand. She met the scrutiny of the three soldiers and their blasters. They had the drop on her. Even if she got one blade loose, they'd fill her full of holes before she got the others off. While fighting to get her breath back—her ears ringing from the blow—she looked into the mean eyes of her aggressors, waiting for their move.

The rumble SA had started in the transmitter room continued to gallop towards them, but the soldiers seemed more concerned with her than the shredding death rushing at their backs. The rear-most of the group then looked behind. Despite being in the sights of the other two, she copied the third soldier and looked past them at the cloud of stalt dust filling the far end of the corridor.

When the white swell drew closer, the other two soldiers finally turned to see it. SA scrabbled to her feet, spun around, and sprinted away from them. Although vulnerable with her back exposed, the soldiers now had far more to worry about than taking her down.

Just before she vanished from sight, SA looked back at the soldiers again. They were running after her, or rather, they were running in the same direction as her to get away from the dust cloud. It moved like a force of nature, not yielding to anything. If they didn't get out of the way, it would roll right over them and turn their skin to paste.

Another sharp left and then right, SA couldn't hear the soldier's clumsy getaway anymore, just the bellow of crashing stalt. Maybe it had already consumed them.

The next turn led SA into a hangar, the bright sun blinding her momentarily from where it shone through the large open exit at the far end. It turned every surface into a mirror, but she pushed on, blinking in an attempt to regain her sight.

The transmitter room had been vast, but the hangar dwarfed it by comparison. At least six times the size, it had a tall ceiling that looked like it stretched as high as the palace itself, twenty metres tall, if not more. There were soldiers everywhere, but none of them noticed SA. Even if they had, they were too busy saving their own lives to care.

SA watched a ship fly out into the bright desert. It looked like one of the first to get free. A small fighter, something about it demanded her attention. When a large chrome mech followed behind, her frame sank. Reyes and Sparks—she'd missed them.

Over the rumble of the collapsing palace, SA then heard more soldiers burst into the hangar through the door she'd just entered. They saw her before they saw the ships. The trio she'd just gotten away from led the group. They levelled their blasters at her for a second time.

# CHAPTER 3

Where the group in the corridor had only been three strong, they now headed up a squad of over twenty beings. For a second, SA paused and stared at them. Despite their attempts to kill her, it lifted her heart to see they'd made it. Enemy or not, no being deserved to be torn to shreds by the collapsing palace. Then she focused on the blasters aimed at her, not only from the front three, but those behind them too.

As the swell of the falling palace grew louder, SA stepped back a pace. A moment later, the first signs of the chalky rush raced in on the heels of the army. After she'd watched them all look behind, she took the opportunity and ran. Better to try to avoid blaster fire than wait for the suffocating cloud. At least she had a chance against the soldiers' blasters.

The rest of the ships were lined up against one wall about twenty metres away. A few half-hearted shots came at SA—which her zigzagging run helped her avoid—but she kept her attention on the vessels. One of them would get her out of there.

The smell of exhaust fumes and fuel filled the air, and the roar of more and more engines starting erupted as SA scanned the still-parked ships. The second she saw one she recognised, she'd get into it. With no Sparks to hot-wire them, she had to pick one she didn't need a fingerprint or a key to start, and one she knew how to fly. Although—with an army so large and with an undoubtedly high turnover of troops—maybe none of them needed identification to get into the sky. It would be an expensive task to have to modify them so frequently, so why would Enigma bother? Also, she might not find one she recognised, so she'd have to try her luck. If she could fly one ship, she could fly them all. At least, she hoped she could.

The rip and smash of the collapsing palace drew so close the rumble of it shook the ground. SA continued on her dodging run, the stress of her sudden changes in direction hurting her knees. Would the next turn be one too many? She gave up and ran straight. If any soldiers were still focused on her, the falling building would crush them in the next few seconds anyway.

The line of ships ranged in size. Some looked like they could take an entire army millions of light-years away. Some looked like they'd need refuelling every half an hour. If SA had any hope of getting out of there alive, she needed a good balance of both. She needed to be nimble, and she needed to get off-world.

One of the blasts from behind ran so close to SA it dazzled her, momentarily giving her blind spots in her peripheral vision. She heard the hiss when it singed her hair, and ruffled her nose against the strong stench of it.

Now just metres between SA and the ships, the sound of boosters, laser fire, and structural ruin made her head spin. She checked behind to see how many of the army still fired at her. Half of them had already been consumed by rolling dust, but a few blasts still burst from the cloud. Then the sound of destruction entered the hangar, and the laser fire stopped.

SA paused to watch the cracks streak away from the door frame she and the army had just entered through. Like reverse lightning, an explosion of fault lines raced up the wall, forking and growing wider as they went, moving faster than she could trace them.

When many of the cracks reached the ceiling, the wall leaned forward. A cumbersome titan, the large lump of stalt slowly fell.

The screams of dying and scared creatures added to the insanity around her. Nothing SA could do for them now, she took off again in the direction of the ships. Then she saw the cracks in the wall behind the vessels … The destruction had caught up with her.

While clenching her jaw as if it would help her find more energy, SA doubled her pace, until she saw she had no chance of getting there in time. Better to stand back than be buried beneath a mountain of stalt, even if it did mean not getting to a ship. Like she'd just seen with the wall behind the army shooting at her, the cracks stretched from floor to ceiling. Large chunks of crystal fell onto the ships first, the rest of the wall tumbling down behind it.

Beings screamed, the rumble of rocks smashed down, and ships' engines roared with the need to get out of there. For a second, the white dust gathered at the bottom of the wall as if building momentum, then rushed towards SA. Because she'd seen it coming, she had the good sense to hold her breath. After a deep inhale, she pursed her lips tight. The dense cloud of dust was thick enough to choke her on its own. Who knew what the sharp stalt particles would do if she breathed them in? Probably turn her lungs to liquid.

Driven back a couple of steps because of the choking rush, SA realised her one major error too late to do anything about it. She hadn't given the same consideration to her eyes that she had to her lungs; instantly blinded by the white cloud, her world suddenly turned black.

# CHAPTER 4

Despite her best efforts to avoid inhaling the dust, SA found it impossible; there was simply too much of it. She coughed and spluttered, the grit leaving a taste of lime in her mouth. But the darkness plaguing her sight had lightened. For what good it would do her.

The sound of the crumbling palace swirled around SA. Destruction came at her from every angle. Blinded and over-whelmed by the chaos, she barely knew which way was up. It drove her to inaction, rooting her to the spot.

The air clearer for now, SA drew several deep and wheezy breaths. It helped to settle her ragged pulse and straighten her thoughts. She looked in the direction of where she knew the hangar's exit to be, at least where she *hoped* it to be. The brightest spot around, it must be coming from where the sun bounced off the stalt desert. She couldn't do anything about someone trying to shoot her, but she could at least try to run out of there. From the cacophony of insanity around her, she probably didn't have to worry about being gunned down anyway. It sounded like most of the creatures were more concerned with their own survival than anything else.

The sound of destruction spurred SA on. No other option but to run, she faced the large blurry light that she hoped to be the exit to the hangar and broke into a sprint. Every blind step could be the one that tripped her, her stomach lurching in anticipation of a fall. She pushed through her desire to slow down. Whether she took her time or not, she wouldn't be able to find her way any more easily. At least speed gave her a better chance of getting out of there.

Something then crashed into SA's side, sending her several wobbly steps to the left before she fell to her knees. No give in the hard stalt ground, the shock of her landing ran fire from her patellae, up the insides of both thighs, and into her stomach with nauseating precision.

The deep cracking around her ran a vibration through the ground as it drew closer again. Although far fewer than before, the sound of whining engines swelled through the chaos. It sounded like the remaining few were getting out of there. Everyone else was done for—including her.

SA jumped back to her feet again and ran at the light. She couldn't give up. Not that she expected a response, but she tried anyway. *Seb? Reyes? Sparks? Bruke?* If Bruke had even gotten out of there. Poor Bruke. Her sense already told her what the lack of reaction confirmed: no one could hear her. As much as disappointment tugged on her tired frame, she wouldn't let it beat her. She dragged speed from deep inside, gritted her teeth, and screamed. It helped her push through the pain, exhaustion, and confusion.

Another loud splash of falling stalt behind, the wind it created crashed into the back of SA. It felt like half the hangar had dropped. At least she was ahead of it; silver linings and all that. A second later, the linings were left behind as the cloud of dust rushed forward and smothered her, choking her with its dry grip. She held her breath and kept moving.

This time SA saw the being coming from her left and stopped before it crashed into her. No more than a silhouette in her grey-toned world, it ran across where she would have been had she not halted. Although she noticed the one at her left, she had no chance of seeing the one behind. When it slammed into her, her head snapped back before she got flung forwards.

After several unsteady steps—her arms windmilling—SA managed to keep her balance. The second she picked up to full speed again, her big toe connected with something hard and immovable on the ground. The pain she'd felt in her knees had nothing on the sharp rod of fire that streaked up her foot, snapping a hard spasm through it that even made the strong structure of her boots yield.

Another crash-landing, her already sore palms paid the price for softening her fall again. A large, hard, and calloused foot then stamped on the back of her right hand as it ran past. Although it stung, SA knew the shoeless creature hadn't broken anything. Thank the stars it didn't have boots on.

Spurred on by the devastation behind her, SA jumped to her feet again. Despite the hard pulsating throb in her toe, she picked up her speed until she moved at a sprint. Silhouettes all around her, she sensed she'd become part of the mass and final exodus from that side of the palace. Anything left behind wouldn't be getting out of there.

And then light. It opened up around her, seeming to give her a clear view of things despite her blindness. While panting to recover, SA inhaled the fresh Varna air. Even her very first breath brought some relief to her tight and dust-filled lungs. Another deep inhale and she coughed hard, the metallic taste of blood lifting up onto the back of her tongue.

After she'd swallowed it down with the stalt's taste of lime, SA looked up in the direction of what must have been the sun. She felt the warm press of it as she listened to the structure collapse behind her in a damn near deafening crash. For the briefest moment, she allowed herself the smallest of smiles. She'd made it.

# CHAPTER 5

I t took for SA to step outside to appreciate just how loud it had been in the hangar. The screams and cries from the grieving soldiers still rang out around her, but now they had no ceiling to both contain their grief and throw it back at them as if mocking their plight. The final crash of the falling structure had removed the groans, pops, and cracks that had ripped through the palace like a prophet of doom heralding an extinction-level event.

A ringing in her ears—which hadn't entirely left her since she'd set the leveller off—SA turned on the spot as if she'd see something other than whiteness, but everywhere looked the same, especially now the silhouette of the palace had gone with its collapse. She could make out the movement of beings around her, and nothing more. Not even their forms were entirely visible; they were just grey blobs of varying sizes. In the chaos of their panic, they moved without rhyme or reason. The mass exodus clearly ended outside the palace. Now they'd fled, they didn't know where to go beyond that.

It would be a complete waste of time, but SA did it anyway. *Seb? Reyes? Sparks? Bruke?* None of them replied to her. It took for that moment for her to realise the sound of the ships had gone too. The traffic in the sky had already moved on, either fled or downed; hopefully, her friends were safe. When she looked up, her sight turned whiter than ever.

As SA's already rapid pulse quickened, she rode out her heavy breaths and continued to turn on the spot until she felt dizzy. In an attempt to ease the ringing in her ears, she opened and closed her mouth. It had no effect. Blind and helpless, her spinning only served to confuse her more. Now she'd lost where she came from, she had no idea where to go. What a moron. "Damn it."

"Oi, you!"

The words ran ice through SA's veins and her shoulders snapped taut. It didn't matter that she couldn't see, she knew they were addressing her, but she didn't reply. There seemed little point; they'd reveal what they wanted soon enough. From the sound of their voice, she'd say they were desperate to do it.

Even with the noises of the survivors around her, SA still heard footsteps approaching. It sounded like maybe five or six beings at the most. No doubt they were soldiers still fighting for their cause.

"You're one of them," the deep voice of a few seconds ago said. It sounded like it belonged to a beast of a creature, a baseline delivered from what could have only been a cavernous diaphragm.

At first she nearly denied it, shaking her head before she spoke. But there seemed little reason to. Instead, she took one final deep breath and tried to centre herself. A few metres between her and the creatures coming towards her, she clenched and raised her fists, widened her stance, and faced the direction of the speaker.

The beast with the deep voice laughed. "And there's me thinking you'd come in without a fight. I mean, I might be wrong, but it looks like you can't see anything. Otherwise you'd see the two guards approaching you from behind."

When SA spun around, the realisation hit her slightly later than the punch to the back of her head. It struck the bell in her skull and added a flash to the white dominating her vision. The beast behind shoved her forwards. She tripped, fell, and landed on her already sore knees and palms.

Before SA could do anything, one of the creatures kicked her so hard in the stomach it drove the air from her body. On all fours, she coughed and gasped for air before another creature kicked her from the side, flipping her over so she landed on her back.

Despite being dizzy from the beating, when SA looked up, she saw with slightly more definition than before. Silhouettes, clearer than they'd been a moment ago, even with the bright sun behind them. A quick count showed her five creatures. When she saw the next one take a two-step run up, she rolled out of its way before it could connect. As it kicked air, she brought her leg around and swiped its standing foot. The beast hit the ground hard, but before it had a chance to yell out, she climbed over it and plunged a knife into the top of its head with a definitive crunch. She buried the blade up to the hilt. The beast's muscles relaxed beneath her as she withdrew her knife and climbed off it.

At least two of the remaining four soldiers hissed at her. She also heard a throaty growl and the snapping of strong jaws. The blade raised and ready to fight, the warm trickle of the creature's blood ran over the hilt and rode down the peaks and valleys made by the fingers of her tight grip.

If the creatures had any fighting experience, they didn't show it. They stood shoulder to shoulder in front of her—a neat line ready to be taken down. Maybe they took her blindness to be complete.

The one with the deep voice spoke again. "You got lucky. It's not going to happen again if you try to fight the rest of us. Give up now and we'll let you live."

Because of her slightly better view, SA managed to link the

voice to the tallest of her attackers. The knife's grip slick in her right hand, she loosed it, heard the gasp of a clean hit in the beast's neck, and watched the silhouette fold while the life gargled out of it. The others froze, and before they had time to recover, she threw three more knives at them. Each one hit the head of one of the silhouettes. Each one dropped its target.

For the next few seconds, SA stood still and listened. If any of the group remained, she couldn't see them. While she had to keep her wits—her giddy pulse goading her to take action—she could only fight what she knew to be there.

SA let some of the tension leave her body with a long exhale while she slowly turned around again. No silhouettes close to her. The same white view as before, she didn't know which direction to head in. But she had to make a decision. A group of five had been easy enough to defeat with partial sight; if a larger squad approached her, she had no chance.

# CHAPTER 6

The first SA knew of being shot at came when a pulse of laser fire hit the ground next to her. Shattered stalt peppered her left shin. Then another shot hit, no closer, but on her right this time.

Still turning and trying to make her mind up, she didn't know which way to run. Because of the noise of beings all around her, she had no idea where the shots came from. Another blast hit the ground; this time behind her. The spray of stalt chips smashed against her calves.

Then it dawned on her: the glare of the sun. Of course! Why had it taken her so long? The brightest of all the bright spots, it was what she'd followed to get out of the hangar. If she travelled towards it again, it would take her away from where the palace had been and, hopefully, the bulk of the soldiers too.

Like she'd done when escaping the hangar, she took off and moved at a jog, totally unaware of what lay in her path. The same lurch in her stomach with every step, but like with the guards, she couldn't avoid what she couldn't see. Deal with the problems as she clattered into them. Who needed palms and kneecaps anyway?

Yet another blast crashed into the ground on her right. It felt like the shots were coming from behind her.

Despite the blaster fire—several more shots missing SA but clearly aimed her way—it didn't sound like anything chased her as she ran. The accuracy of the attack backed up her theory, the shots missing by wider margins the farther she travelled. Whatever was trying to kill her had a half-hearted lust for it at best; maybe they weren't even aiming for her.

Not only did the accuracy of the shots deteriorate, but they came less frequently too. As SA tuned into her own laboured breaths from where she tried to keep a good pace despite her exhaustion, she realised they'd turned into the dominant sound now rather than the chaos that had surrounded her. Rightly or wrongly, she slowed down to a fast walk. The limited evidence she had told her she didn't have to worry about being chased. The bigger threat now came from her inability to see. One foot in front of the other, she gave herself the time she needed to plant down and be certain of its stability before she took her next step. Blind, exhausted, emotionally frayed, and confused, the slower pace felt like a luxury, and until she knew she couldn't afford it, she'd damn well take it.

While maintaining her fast march, SA rolled her shoulders and snapped her head from side to side. No twinges or major pains yet, but they'd come. She'd written her body a lengthy IOU. Give it a day or two and she'd be aching from head to toe.

Despite the bright sun, the strong wind kept the temperature down. Such a fierce glare in front of her, even mostly blind, SA had to squint in the face of it.

The sounds behind grew more distant, yet SA still had a desire to run. But she ignored it. The evidence at that moment told her she had nothing chasing her. With her struggles as heightened as they already were, she didn't need to add to them by running away from imagined foes.

Now she'd slowed down—her throat dry and her muscles tired—questions flooded SA's mind. She'd gotten away from the immediate danger, but what now? How wide did the desert stretch? Would she be walking until she dropped? Would her sight return? What kind of creatures lived out in the stalt landscape? A shake of her head helped her stop the thoughts. One step at a time. Safety first, and then she'd plan her next move. At some point, the Shadow Order would come looking for her. They had to, right?

How the thing approached her without her hearing she didn't know, but when a heavy step slammed down on her left, SA spun to face it while drawing two knives from her harness. Like with the soldiers, the thing then attacked her from the other side. A whoosh on her right gave her the slightest of warnings for the thick tail, or rope, or whatever it was that crashed into the side of her head. She went down hard.

For the few seconds SA remained conscious, she felt hairy and muscular arms grip her, wrap some kind of rope around her, and throw her over its shoulder. Despite trying to fight it, her head turned increasingly woozy, and as the thing carried her away, the whiteness dominating her vision turned black.

# CHAPTER 7

The cold rush hit SA square in the face, bringing her to with a sharp gasp. It forced an involuntary inhale, which dragged some of the water into her lungs. While listening to her own barking panic, she shook and twisted to get free, but the ropes were tied too tight. Restraints at her wrists and ankles, she'd been bound in a sitting position to a chair she couldn't see.

SA's inability to move accelerated her panic. Her pulse pounded through her skull as she tried to look around, but they'd tied a blindfold on her as well.

Slowly, SA relaxed, dragging more air in with each breath. Her throat was sore, dry, and tight, but slightly looser than before. As she found the rhythm of her respiration, her pulse slowed and the tension in her chest relaxed. On what felt like her first full inhale, another splash of cold water slammed into her face, the force of it knocking her head back. At least this time she had the good sense to hold her breath.

The water dripped from SA's face, soaking her already damp chest. "Where am I?"

Whatever had given her the drenching remained in front of her. She could feel the slight cool from being in its shadow and hear its breaths as a deep rattle. But the creature offered her no reply.

SA swallowed, a dry pinch of dehydration tickling her oesophagus. "Who are you? What do you want with me?" Her frustration got the better of her and she spoke through a clamped jaw. "Where. Am. I?"

But the creature gave her nothing, and although she waited for another splash of water, that didn't come either.

SA DIDN'T KNOW HOW LONG SHE'D BEEN ASLEEP FOR, BUT THE cold press of something against her lips woke her instantly. She clamped them shut and shook her head, twisting away from the cool pressure. While breathing through her nose, she tried to take in the scent of what was being offered to her. Other than a musky tang of sweat from the hand around the cup, she smelled nothing.

Although SA couldn't have seen the creature when it knocked her down, she'd caught a glimpse of its silhouette. In her memory, it stood considerably taller than her. It confirmed her impression of it when it spoke, its voice so deep, the vibration of it shook SA's chest. "Drink."

SA turned away from the cup. "Who are you? And how do I know it's safe to drink?"

The thing pressed the cup harder against her lips, stopping just before it hurt. It had the force to push her teeth out if it tried, and if it came to a battle of wills, there would only be one winner, so SA took a sip. Cool and fresh, it tasted like water, her throat relaxing for the liquid relief. "I don't understand. It seems like you're trying to take care of me. If that's the case, why do I have a blindfold on? Why am I tied to a chair?"

But the creature didn't respond. Instead, it let out a deep sigh while standing up. SA then listened to the thud of its steps as it walked away from her.

A GENTLE TOUCH ON HER SHOULDER ROUSED SA. THE BEST WAY she'd been awakened so far. Then, as if to rectify that, another hard splash of water slammed into her face. She held her breath while it ran down her front, turning her top sodden, the damp fabric cold against her chest.

SA flinched at the next splash of water and turned away so most of it hit the side of her face.

The beast's words came out as a furious boom. "Hold still!"

SA snapped rigid and faced it. Despite the fight burning deep inside her, she knew how to pick her battles.

Maybe the creature felt bad about shouting at her, because the next soaking came from the beast pouring water on her rather than slamming her in the face with it. The action bordered on nurturing. SA felt the warmth of its breath against her face and listened to its slow respiration as it concentrated on the task at hand. When the flow of water stopped, the same smell of sweat on the beast's skin smothered her from its close proximity. The gentler approach threw her off. What did this creature want with her?

THE BRUTE GENTLY TAPPED THE TOP OF SA'S HEAD TO WAKE HER up. Where she'd expected pain from being tied to a chair for so long and what she'd been through prior to being made this thing's prisoner, she felt none.

The creature washed her eyes again. Tender like it had been previously.

"What's going on?" SA said to it. "Please tell me. Who are you? What are you doing to me? How long have I been here?" She then added, "And thank you for being more gentle this time."

But the beast didn't respond.

When SA heard the sound of a ship's engine nearby, she jumped and looked in the direction of the noise. Not that she could see anything with the blindfold across her eyes. "What's that? Who's there?" A million and one possibilities sat at the edge of her mind. Something had come to take her away. The beast had nursed her back to health before selling her off as a slave. What would they use her for? The fighting pits? Prostitution? She levelled her breathing. It wouldn't help to panic about it. She could only deal with what got put in front of her.

As before, the creature responded with silence, adding fuel to the paranoid fire raging inside SA's skull.

The ship's engine then shut off, the creature moved away from SA, and after a few minutes of silence, she accepted she'd been left alone. Again.

SA's MOST RECENT SOAKING GAVE TEETH TO THE NIGHT's SHARP chill. The cold sting of her damp top pressed against her chest, and gooseflesh lifted on her arms. She shivered where she sat. If she stayed there much longer, she'd get pneumonia—at least, that was what common sense told her—but deep down, although cold, she felt great in every other respect.

The creature in front of her, SA opened her mouth to question it again, but it spoke first. "I'm going to take your blindfold off in a second. You've been here for three days, which should be enough time to heal. I'm hoping your sight will be fully restored. I'm doing this at night because you've had that blindfold on for a long time. To take it off in the bright glare of the Varna desert will just turn you blind again. We can let your sight wake up with the new day. Are you ready?"

SA nodded.

The chink of the creature putting the bucket of water down against the stalt ground, it then walked around behind her and untied the knot in the blindfold at the back of her head. The soft and damp fabric fell down her chest and landed in her lap.

While blinking repeatedly, SA made out the glow of a nearby fire. Everywhere else looked dark, but as she blinked against the blur, her world shifted into a tighter focus. At first, silhouettes appeared as her world began to wake up.

Not yet perfect, but her sight better than it had been since the stalt dust got into her eyes, SA remained tied to the chair. She looked left and right for the creature holding her captive. It stood too far behind for her to see. When it walked around her right side, she turned to look up at it and gasped.

# CHAPTER 8

A beast unlike any SA had seen before. The thing looked like a cross between a centaur and a gorilla. A chest as wide as SA stood tall, it had four arms and four legs. Although where a centaur would have the lower body of a horse, this creature had the lower body of a sabre-toothed tiger but bigger. Much bigger. A tail thicker than one of SA's arms, no wonder it had knocked her out cold on the first attempt.

The creature's mouth stretched so wide it could have easily removed SA's torso at the waist with one bite. Its sharp and jagged teeth were crammed in like rocks at the foot of a cliff and leaned back towards its throat. If it latched on to something, it would only let go when it wanted to. To stare into the darkness of its gullet forced an involuntary gulp from her.

Still bound to her chair, SA shook and twisted. At least if she could fight the thing, she'd have a chance. But the struggle proved as ineffective then as it had done for the past few days. The ropes were tied too tight for her to move. A hard clench to her jaw, she said, "You coward. Tying me up so you can eat me. Look at the size of you, and you won't even make it a fair fight."

The beast had yellowed claws on the ends of its thick fingers. It swung for her, the sharp enamel flying across the front of her face, the wind from the action disturbing her hair.

Instead of the sharp sting and then warm rush of blood from the cut it opened up on her, SA felt the ropes around her loosen and fall to the stalt ground. Almost impressed by its ability to swing so close and not cut her, she flinched when it threw several more swipes, each one so quick they were easier to feel than see. The pressure loosened and the ropes fell free from her wrists and ankles.

After rolling her shoulders to shrug off her bonds, SA got to her feet. The action felt easier than it should have. No aches or pains like she'd expected, especially after the kicking she'd received when she got free from the palace. She stared at the brute, clenched her jaw, and balled her fists. No matter that she didn't fancy her chances, she wouldn't go down without a fight. If the creature planned on killing her, she needed to leave a lasting impression on it if nothing else.

But the beast didn't make a move. It simply regarded her through its blood-red glare.

"Are you going to try to eat me now?" she said.

A hard scowl hooded the brute's crimson focus as it glowered at her for a few more seconds. Then its expression changed; twisting at first, it opened its split-jawed mouth, threw its head back, and laughed at the sky. The deep boom of it rolled like distant thunder.

It took at least thirty seconds before the brute stopped laughing at her. When it did, it shook its head. "Of course not. We ravas are all herbivores."

The tension left SA's frame as if it were liquid seeping from her toes. Her ability to articulate herself went with it and she spoke with a stammer. "W-w-with jaws like that?"

The beast picked up a large stalt rock and threw it into its wide mouth. When it bit down, the sides of its muscular jaw widened by a few inches. It instantly turned the rock to pebbles, many of which spilled over its bottom lips and fell to the ground while it chewed.

SA nodded and smiled to herself. "Okay, that makes sense now." As she sat back on the seat she'd been strapped to, she said, "So why did you knock me out and tie me up if you mean me no harm?"

"I did it for your own good."

Hard not to laugh, SA shook her head at the thing. "Huh?"

"Well, your own good *and* my own good. I could see you were a kind person and probably on our side. I watched you run out of the palace and saw you fight those guards despite being blind. I may be big, but after seeing you in the full flow of battle, I didn't fancy my chances if it turned sour, so I had to take you down before you could attack me. I'm not sure I would have been able to persuade you to come with me otherwise. I couldn't risk getting into a fight with you."

As much as SA wanted to deny the assumption, she couldn't.

"When I got you back here and confirmed you were blinded because of stalt dust, I needed to make sure you didn't rub your eyes. You had so much of it in them, any pressure would have turned your eyeballs to liquid."

SA flinched at the thought.

"To make you better, I had to treat your eyes. To treat your eyes, I had to tie you up and blindfold you with that."

Following the line to where the thing pointed, SA looked down at what had been her blindfold. It had felt like fabric, but she now saw it was a large thin leaf. "What is it?"

"It's the fahar plant. It grows on the banks of this lake."

So preoccupied with her captor up until that point, SA hadn't looked around. Now the creature mentioned it, she turned to take in the vast lake behind her. Although she could see small campfires dotted around it, they were too far away for her to tell what beings had lit them. The bright moon reflected off the water that looked to stretch for miles in every direction. Were it not for the wind disturbing the surface of it, it would have been hard to distinguish from the stalt ground.

"This lake and the fahar plant have healing qualities. We have just two sources of water on Varna. Two lakes of almost equal size. This one, which breeds life, and the one at the planet's other pole, which only brings death. It's like the planet filters all the poison into the other lake so it can deliver purified water to this one."

"Why didn't you explain all of this to me at the time?"

"I didn't know I could trust you."

"And you do now?"

"I'm not sure, but I knew you'd be healed by now, so I had to."

She took another look at the beast's large and clawed hands. If it wanted to, it could clamp a grip on the top of SA's head and turn her skull to dust with one squeeze. However, despite its appearance, it held itself like a peaceful being. Its muscles were at ease, powerful if it needed them, but not primed and ready to be used. This creature only acted in self-defence. It clearly had no interest in going to war. A few more seconds of silence between them, she frowned at the thing in front of her. "And what do you want from me?"

"Nothing."

When SA didn't respond, the creature elaborated. "Enigma landed here several years ago. We should have taken them down then, but it's not in our nature. Also, we didn't anticipate what they were capable of. We're a simple and democratic species. It's hard for us to understand the mind and actions of a dictatorship. When they first came here, they had a few ships and weapons, but most beings in the galaxy have a few ships and weapons. By the time we knew we needed to take action, they were too large for us to take down. Their industry—from training soldiers, to making weapons, to building their palace—has been massively detrimental to our ecosystem. They output pollution at a frightening rate. At least, they did."

"But you have the toxic lake for that, right?"

"We did. But they make too much for it to cope with. We visit the black lake regularly and it's overloaded. If Enigma hadn't been stopped, that pollution would have spilled over into this lake and turned our water source toxic. We'd all—"

"Die," SA finished for him in a whisper.

"Exactly. You and your friends took down Enigma. Without realising it, you saved us."

At the mention of her friends, SA perked up. "Do you know what's happened to the others I came here with?"

While releasing a deep sigh, the creature shook its head. "Gone."

The word plummeted as a lead weight through SA's stomach and she could barely repeat what she'd heard. "*Gone?*"

The beast wrung its hands while frowning at her. "I'm *so* sorry." Before SA responded, it added, "But we've brought a ship over so you can get off the planet. It's one of Enigma's vessels. I'm not sure they'll be needing it now."

SA had pulled back into herself, and although she had an awareness of replying to the beast, she couldn't help but focus on the word *gone.* "No, I suppose you're right."

"I'm afraid we have no idea where your friends are, but at least you can try to find them, right?"

It started as a smile that quickly turned into a laugh. The creature watched her with a deep frown. "When you said gone," she said, "I thought you meant *gone* gone."

The creature clapped a hand to its mouth as it gasped. Its eyes wide, it said, "I'm *sorry*. I can see that now. No, we think they're still alive. They're just not on Varna anymore."

SA then watched the creature turn around and crouch down. When it stood back up again, it had a plate of food in its hands. "Here, have this; you need it. When you're done, we'll get you off this planet so you can go and find your friends."

# CHAPTER 9

S A cut her splice root in two, speared one half of the yellow-sprouting vegetable with her fork, and put it in her mouth. It had a slightly bitter taste that caused some of the muscles in her neck to tighten as she chewed, but she could tolerate it. Besides, vegetables weren't supposed to be enjoyed, just digested so she could eat the rest of her meal guilt-free. She swallowed her mouthful, her throat sore from having spoken so much.

While sipping her cool and fresh water, SA looked at the others. They all stared back like they expected her to tell more of her story: Sparks, Reyes, Bruke, Moses, and Seb. It had been several weeks since they'd come back from Varna, this being the first time they'd all managed to get together again to catch up. Instead of giving them what she thought they wanted, she put the second half of the splice root into her mouth.

"And that's when you came to the Shadow Order's base?" Moses said.

To avoid speaking with a mouthful, SA covered the lower half of her face with her hand and nodded.

The warmth of Seb's grip in hers never got old, so when he

reached over, SA responded and they held hands beneath the table.

Bruke glowed to look at them both, his eyes glistening with backed-up tears. "And then you came here?"

Again SA nodded.

"Oh, how I would have loved to see that."

While rolling her eyes, Sparks said, "I'm sure they were grateful to have that moment alone, Bruke. Besides, you may have wanted to see it"—she spoke in a quieter voice, faking conspiracy—"but the neighbours said these two howled at the sky for days. They were like rutting bullwats."

Heat lifted on SA's cheeks and she dropped her attention to her dinner plate.

After a few seconds of silence, Reyes cleared her throat, sparing SA's embarrassment. "Um, I suppose seeing as SA's told you her story, and seeing as we're all together for what could be the last time in a while, I owe you all an explanation."

One of the most composed beings SA had met, she watched the now vulnerable Reyes. Her eyes shifted as she looked for the approval of those around her to continue.

It took for Sparks to break the silence. "*The Faradis*?"

Reyes drew a deep breath. It looked like she went into herself, finding the strength from deep inside to keep talking. She finally nodded. "Yep." She then winced to take in her friends again. "If you all want to hear it, that is …"

Sparks tutted and threw her hands in the air. "Of course! We've all heard about *The Faradis*, but none of us have had a first-hand account. It sounded like one hell of a thing to go through."

After several nods as if to get herself going, Reyes finally said, "No story could come close to the reality of it."

Her words sucked all the air from the room. SA stopped chewing.

"It all started when we were on the *Crimson Destroyer*, our mothership. We'd not long been back from a mission. A horrible mission on a sandy planet called Q328. Because of that experience, they'd sent all of the ranking officers on a break. They held the rookies back because they worried we'd not cope if we spent time on our own. There had been too many rookie suicides in the past. The plan was to stay on board for a few weeks before we went on any other jobs. We were officially *off-duty*." She laughed and shook her head. When she pulled her hair from her face, SA noticed her shaking hand. "But best-laid plans and all that …"

A slight glaze covered Reyes' eyes when she looked up at the rest of them. Seb let go of SA's hand and reached out to the Hispanic Marine. He touched the back of her arm and spoke with soft tones. "You don't need to go through this again if you're not ready."

"I'm not sure I'll ever be ready." Before Seb could reply, she said, "But it's time for me to tell it." After a deep inhale to settle herself, she said, "I remember when it came onto our radar. We were playing murderball—"

"*Murderball?*" Bruke said.

"You have a small metal ball you have to throw into your opponents' goal. Other than that, there are no rules …"

# CHAPTER 10

Reyes ran on Patel's flank, open for the ball, ready should he need to offload it. Sweat burned her eyes, but she dared not blink; she didn't have time to blink.

Quick feet and fast straight-line speed, Patel was the star player on their team. It took everything Reyes had to shadow him.

Chan suddenly appeared to their right. Even with the distance between them, she had a good chance of catching up. The fastest of all the Marines and on the opposite team, the small woman of Chinese American descent had thighs like a cheetah and could catch a rocket on take-off.

Heading straight for Patel, Chan would catch him if Reyes didn't do something to stop her. With no rules in murderball other than get the ball in the opponents' net, she gritted her teeth and dug deep. In a burst of speed she didn't think she had in her, she charged at Chan. Because the small Marine had her focus on Patel, she didn't notice Reyes soon enough.

Reyes hit Chan with a hard shoulder barge, driving an *oomph* from her. The blow lifted the small Marine from her feet, shoving her away from them and keeping Patel's route to the goal clear.

Patel turned to Reyes and nodded his thanks. A greater luxury than blinking, it made him miss Hicks' approach.

"Man on!" Reyes gasped, but Patel turned too late and Hicks slammed into him.

Because she'd seen Hicks coming, Reyes jumped aside, dodging the pair as they went down. They were heading for a collision with the metal wall on their left, but Patel managed to release the ball in time, delivering it directly to Reyes' grip.

A tight clench on the small metal sphere, Reyes felt twenty pairs of eyes turn her way. It lit the touchpaper, her system flooding with adrenaline as she took off again. Quicker than before, she made a beeline for the opposing team's goal.

Whoever decided to build the sports arena next to the *Crimson Destroyer*'s huge boosters clearly hadn't done exercise before. More sweat than ever ran into her eyes as Reyes swallowed against the dryness in her throat while gulping in the baked air.

The small red metal murderball in one hand, Reyes ran straight at Weston. She slammed her palm into the centre of his face and felt his nose crunch. Before he hit the floor, she jumped over him without breaking stride.

The hard surfaces in the arena picked up the sound of the others. It told Reyes all she needed to know without her looking back. If she didn't reach the goal soon, she'd be hit by a stampede.

Patel, having done most of the work, watched as only Julius stood between Reyes and the goal. A woman larger than many of the men, she wouldn't drop to a handoff like Weston just had.

Reyes darted left, sending Julius diving before she shifted back to the right. As the Marine fell, clasping at thin air where she'd expected Reyes to be, it gave her a clear run on goal. An open net only a metre away from her, she threw the ball hard to the satisfying blare of the buzzer as it crashed home.

They'd won! Reyes threw her arms in the air. She didn't

normally score. A defender, she'd seen the opportunity to follow Patel and took it. While jumping up and down on the spot, she cheered. The rest of her team cheered with her. Then she saw Chan. The game clearly hadn't ended for her.

Too late to react, Reyes took the full weight of Chan's shoulder in her stomach. Not quick enough to tense, she went down like a bag of air. The metal floor did nothing to cushion her fall, a skeleton-altering clatter running through her as she took the weight of both of them. When the back of her head slammed down, her world spun and she fought to remain conscious.

As Reyes found her bearings, Chan got to her feet and loomed over her. Eyes wild, she licked her lips and paced back and forth. An animal over its kill, the glaze in her green stare showed she'd lost herself to the adrenaline rush.

Although Reyes opened her mouth to speak, Patel's voice cut her off. "What the hell was that, Chan?" It echoed through the large arena.

A scowl as mean as the one she levelled on Reyes, she spun on him and threw her arms in the air. "What do you expect? I couldn't let her score."

Reyes sat up too quickly, her head spinning again. After holding her brow for a few seconds, she pointed her finger at the small Marine. "That's bullshit. You *knew* I'd already scored. You just don't like it that I took you out first."

"Of course I don't. You *cheated!*"

"You were in play! How long have you been playing this game, Chan? You know the rules."

Chan worked her jaw as if chewing gum, her hands on her hips.

The fire slightly calmed in Reyes and she lowered her tone. Because of the silence in the vast hall, her voice still carried. "This was yet another attempt from you to take me down. Like you always do. I still don't know what your problem is. You've had it in for me since day one."

While baring gritted teeth, Chan spoke so quietly, Reyes doubted the others heard her. "Don't be such a victim, daddy's girl. It's tedious hearing the privileged moan about how hard they have it."

Still out of breath from the run and from being knocked down, Reyes got to her feet a little too quickly. The arena spun around her and she rocked on her heels before she found her balance. Unlike Chan, she didn't have a problem with everyone else hearing her. "Face it, Chan; you don't like me, which makes you do whatever you can to hurt me."

Chan stepped close enough for Reyes to smell the sweat on her skin. At five feet exactly, she stood a few inches shorter than Reyes. She looked up at her and continued to speak through clenched teeth, quiet enough to keep her comments between the two of them private again. "You're a little daddy's girl. We got here on merit; *you're* here because Daddy pulled some strings for you."

The same line she'd heard from Chan a million times already, it still raised Reyes' hackles. She lifted her top lip in a snarl, leaning forwards so their sweating foreheads touched as she spoke slow and deliberate words. "You have no idea what I've done."

"What? You think because you got lucky on that one mission that you're a Marine now? It took you so long to work out how to get away that half your squad died. A child would have twigged sooner than you did."

Reyes drove a headbutt into Chan's nose. A loud *crack* rang out and Chan stumbled back several wobbly paces.

The closest of the other Marines was still several metres away. Too far away to stop Chan, who screamed as she charged.

Chan hit Reyes flush, knocking her down. She rained punches

on her as they fell, and continued to pummel her when they hit the floor.

The blows came so quick, Reyes had no other choice but to cover her face. Chan might have been small, but she packed explosive power.

A punch got through and landed flush on Reyes' nose. It sent fire through her sinuses, blinding her with her own tears. Chan continued to attack her, her eyes wide, spittle spraying from her mouth as she screamed a shrill cry.

The back of Reyes' hands burned from where she defended against the attack. Chan would do more damage if she didn't do something to stop her.

Winded, sore, and unable to see through her blurred vision, Reyes thrust her pelvis towards the ceiling, bucking Chan off. She then leapt at her with her right fist raised.

But Reyes never landed her blow. Strong arms gripped her around the waist and dragged her back. She recognised the safe grip of her father before she'd even looked around.

His gruff voice made her flinch when he screamed in her ear, "What the hell are you doing, soldier?"

The sound of his berating snapped everyone else to attention, including Chan, who quickly jumped to her feet.

As the rage left her, Reyes dropped her focus to the metal floor and said, "Nothing. I wasn't doing anything."

The warrant officer repositioned himself so he stood between Reyes and Chan. He looked from one to the other. "Whatever nonsense is going on between you two, it stops now. You got that?"

Reyes nodded, but Chan didn't. It wouldn't ever stop, so why should she lie about it?

"Chan?" the WO said. "Don't make me discipline you."

Tears stood in Chan's eyes and she shook while glaring at

Reyes. She then turned to the senior officer, the same rage boiling in her.

Fists larger than any Reyes had ever seen, when she watched her dad clench them, she winced at the fury she knew he had in him.

But Chan spoke before he flipped, letting her words go with a resigned sigh. "I've got it."

A few tense seconds passed where Chan and the WO stared at one another. The man looked like he expected more. When it didn't come, he shook his head and turned to the rest of the Marines in the arena. "Whatever's just happened here, we've got bigger fish to fry. *Much* bigger fish. Something's just come up, and since it's me and a bunch of no-good rookies, we need to respond to it. All of you get to the briefing room *now*."

Reyes watched her dad as he walked past her. He kept his eyes straight ahead and his shoulders pulled back. Chan followed on his heels and spoke when she got close so only Reyes could hear. "Good job Daddy's bailed you out again, eh? He's saved you from yet another kicking."

After she'd drawn a deep breath and let it go—her cheeks puffing out as she exhaled—Reyes felt Patel's gentle touch on her shoulder. "Ignore her," he said. "Those of us who got away from those creatures on Q328 saw who you are. Chan doesn't know shit."

"She knows I watched a lot of people die. That I didn't work out how to get past those creatures soon enough."

Patel fixed her with his deep brown eyes and Reyes dropped her focus to the floor. "Look at me," he said.

When Reyes looked up, she saw a blurred image of him through her tears. A lump burned in her throat. "Too many died on Q328."

"Of course, but we *all* would have died were it not for you. You were the only one to think of a solution."

"I should have thought of it sooner."

Where Patel's grip had been soft on her shoulder, he now tightened it, giving Reyes a gentle shake as he said, "Stop that!"

After drawing a deep breath, Reyes pushed her pain down again, looked at Patel, and nodded.

"Now, come on," Patel said, "let's get to the briefing room before you piss your dad off more than you already have."

# CHAPTER 11

Two rows of chairs stretched across the wide briefing room. The large area had space for many more, but because they were operating on a skeleton staff, no more needed to be laid out. When Reyes walked in and saw Chan in the front row, her pulse quickened, the increased blood flow aggravating the pain on the back of her hands and across her face.

Because she didn't want to sit next to the small and angry Marine, Reyes opted for the row behind her. She made a line of already seated soldiers stand up to give her access to the spare seats near the wall. Lombardo put a hand on Reyes' shoulder as she passed and looked into her eyes. Several inches taller than her, she swiped her long blonde hair behind one ear while studying her face. "Are you okay?"

Reyes nodded.

"I don't know what Chan's problem is. No one else resents you like she does. It must be hard to rise above it in the face of her aggression, but I think you should. It's the only way to deal with crazy."

After she'd dipped a nod at her friend, Reyes said thank you before continuing to pick her way across to the spare seats. Patel followed her like he often did. Their crash and subsequent experience on Q328 had given the survivors a tighter bond than Reyes had with anyone else except for her dad. Despite him always going harder on her than any of the other rookies, they were always tight. Her relationship with him seemed to be the thing that got under Chan's skin the most.

Once she'd sat down—closer to Chan than she would have liked—Reyes looked at the Chinese American Marine and balled her fists. The throb of her bruises forced her to relax them again. As she drew a deep breath, she looked at Patel, who had his attention on her hands. He then looked up at her and raised his eyebrows. Despite what Lombardo had just said, it took for Patel to back it up before she relaxed. He had her best interests at heart. She needed to be the bigger person and rise above Chan's bullshit. Again! She conceded the point with a nod.

But still none of it made sense. Reyes and Chan had been through training together. They'd gotten on well for the first day or two before it turned sour. Something in Chan changed and she'd spent the past few years trying to understand exactly what. Hell, she'd asked her enough times. Maybe, at first, she didn't realise who Reyes' dad was. She might have been the only person on the *Crimson Destroyer* who didn't.

After the crash on Q328, their relationship had worsened still. Not that Reyes had felt like it in any way, but she returned from that mission a hero. It turned their already rocky relationship positively mountainous.

Most of the time Reyes found it in herself to rise above Chan's attacks, but the more Chan went for her, the deeper she got under her skin. In a strange way, she knew Reyes as well as any of the other Marines did. She saw her insecurities and took great pleasure in making sure Reyes knew she saw them. The second they came back from Q328, Chan noticed the deepest wound of the lot. While there, Reyes had been inside the crashed shuttle and watched many Marines die before she worked out how they could escape the cove. A sharper mind would have found a solution sooner.

While letting go of a hard sigh, Reyes slumped in her seat. The heavy expulsion of air did nothing to drive away the nauseating tug of failure and loss sitting inside her like a tumour. She'd take her guilt to the grave.

Just short of thirty commandos in the briefing room, Reyes watched the final few take their seats on the hard plastic chairs. A room like many others in the *Crimson Destroyer*, it was a cold and bleak gunmetal grey. To look at the surroundings made the hard chair feel harder. She squirmed where she sat, a cold chill snapping a shiver through her. With another look at Patel, who glanced back, she said, "What do you think this is about?"

"I thought you might know."

"Come on, Patel, you've been on a mission with my dad and me. You've seen how he talks to me. If he has something he needs to keep secret, you can guarantee I'll be the absolute last person to know about it. He goes harder on me *because* I'm his daughter."

Despite him witnessing it first-hand on Q328, Patel raised his eyebrows. "He makes a show of going harder on you, but everyone can see how much he loves you."

The slap of the WO's awkward steps entered the room, cutting off Reyes' protests. Most of the Marines in there turned to watch the old vet make his way to the front. Reyes felt Chan watching her.

A grizzled scowl as he surveyed the room, the man held himself like someone who knew their worth to their employer. A maverick, how he presented himself didn't matter because of his experience. In fact, he wore his ruggedness as a hard-won badge of pride. After what he'd given in service, he'd earned the right to look how the hell he liked.

Other than the awkward beat of the officer's gait, the room had fallen silent. The wide eyes of every Marine watched him make his way down the aisle between the seats. As he passed by some of the rookies, they curled away from him and averted their gaze.

He walked to the front before he stopped and faced them. The room watched him in silence. He did a slow scan of all the faces there. He looked from left to right and back again. For every Marine he looked at, his scowl deepened as if each face raised his level of disgust at what sat in front of him. When he spoke, Reyes noticed half of the room jump at his gruff voice. "*This* has come onto our radar."

It took the click of the small remote in his hand before Reyes even realised he had a hold of one. At the press of the button, footage of a ship appeared. It filled the wide screen at the front of the room. Obsidian-like black, it moved slowly, floating in space as if it had no purpose. Comprised of three cylinders that looked like horizontal silos, the largest of the three sat in the centre as what must have been the main part of the ship. The two smaller ones on either side were attached so they sat slightly farther back. Each silo had a conical end as if it would help to cut through space. The backs of the two smaller silos had large boosters on them. It looked like the kind of ship a child would make from used toilet rolls.

As still as the ghostly ship itself, the entire room watched it in silence. As it passed the camera, Reyes read the side of it, her lips mouthing the ship's name, *The Faradis.* It travelled through space like a sleeping whale at the bottom of an ocean. Reyes gulped dry air to watch it.

"We don't know who this ship belongs to or where it's come from," the WO said. "It's not a shape we recognise as being built in any region we know. We've scanned it for life forms and found nothing."

While holding up the remote, he said, "Normally we'd assume the crew had all died out and this ship had been floating for some time. But something about this one doesn't sit right."

The next image he brought up on the screen showed the other side of the ship. From the zoomed-in shot of a row of windows, Reyes saw the red glow of emergency lighting inside. "These lights make us think something has been on here recently. That something has happened to the crew. If the ship had been abandoned for a long time, the lights would be off by now. But like I said, when we ran a heat scan on it, we couldn't find any signs of life."

When Reyes glanced across at Chan again, she met the small Marine's harsh glare. Although she felt the swell of her own aches and bruises, it pleased her to see the blood clinging to Chan's nostrils and the blotchy impact marks on her face. At least she'd gotten a few licks in. Despite her hammering heart, she tried to keep any sign of her emotion from her stare. She didn't care whether Chan was pissed with her or not. Two years was a long time for her to learn not to give a shit anymore.

The warrant officer's voice pulled Reyes' attention back to the front of the room. "If I had my way, we'd be going onto this ship with an experienced team, but it looks like we've been caught with our pants down, so I'm going to have to take some of you on there with me."

He'd as good as said it already, but when he said, "So who wants to come?" Reyes' stomach sank. Could she go on another mission like the one they'd only recently come back from? Could she watch more of the people she cared about die if things went tits up again?

## CHAPTER 12

"You coming?" Patel said to Reyes. Like many of the Marines in the room, he'd gotten to his feet and looked like he wanted to leave.

Her attention on her dad, Reyes shook her head. "I'll catch up with you."

After driving a hard pat against her back, Patel moved off with the others towards the room's exit.

Reyes watched her friend's back for a few seconds. She then scanned the room to find Chan staring straight at her. The same malice she always wore, this time it had a caricature twist to it because of her swollen and puffy eyes. She'd have at least one shiner when it all settled down, hopefully, a matching pair.

Despite the six Marines behind her, Chan stopped dead in the gangway leading out of there. "What are *you* grinning at?" Her voice cut through the low murmur of exiting Marines, and they all stopped to look.

Reyes hadn't realised she'd been smiling. She didn't try to change it now she'd had it pointed out to her.

Chan moved a step closer to Reyes and threw a sharp shrug through her shoulders. "Well?" Several of the Marines behind her leaned around the queue and stared at the small Asian American as if their silent aggression would make her move. They'd have to be more overt than that if they wanted the stubborn woman to get out of their way.

No point in hiding it—especially as she now had an audience —Reyes laughed. "Your face. It looks like I've given you at least one black eye. You'll be looking like a panda in the morning, sweetheart."

Hicks cleared his throat at Chan, who turned to glare at him, tutted, and then returned her attention to Reyes. She pointed at her own face. "You *wish* you did this to me. This is from the game of murderball."

Even in the low light of the briefing room, Reyes watched Chan turn red. It looked like she struggled to hold on to the lie. "*Really?* I didn't see you get any of the ball. I assumed because of that, you weren't in the game much. I thought the only action you saw was when *I* slammed into you to stop you tackling Patel. Oh, and your little outburst after the game had finished and everyone else had lowered their guard."

A tightening of her lips, Chan looked like she was going to reply before Julius shoved her in the back. The tallest Marine there, Julius loomed over her. "Come on, Chan, get out of the way. Stop airing your dirty laundry in public."

"Screw you, Julius."

The full six feet and six inches of Julius' frame swelled. A wall of a woman, her broad shoulders rose when she clenched her fists. Her thick jaw tightened. Her large diaphragm delivered her words with the force of a kick drum. "Stop being a prick, Chan, and *move!*"

Although Chan tutted, some of her tension left her small frame; even she had to accept she couldn't win the argument with Julius. Not many of the Marines there could, including the warrant officer. Despite moving off in the direction of the exit, she continued to glare at Reyes.

Because Chan had taken the time to stop and argue with Reyes, she and the line of Marines behind her were the last ones to leave the room. As the final one walked out, Reyes turned to watch her dad stare into space for a few seconds before he glanced over and raised his eyebrows.

He then walked over to Reyes and sat down beside her, releasing a hard groan as he eased into the seat.

The briefing room also doubled as a cinema during times of rest. It had a screen at the front, rows of seats, and low lighting— perfect for watching movies. For the next few seconds, the pair of them stared ahead like they were watching the latest release. Reyes finally broke the silence. "I don't like the look of this mission."

Never one to reply immediately, her dad waited for a few seconds. He'd always told her the first response was rarely the best one, and he'd learned that the hard way. Impetuous as a child, he'd got himself into a lot of sticky situations of his own making. He finally said, "It'll be fine."

"Thanks for the chat, Dad. I feel better now."

Had Reyes shown such disrespect in front of the other Marines, he would have ripped her a new arsehole. Alone, she was still his little girl. The others never saw this side of him, but from what Patel had just said to her, they all knew it to be there.

"It's an empty ship," her father said. "Something's probably happened to the crew. When we get on board, we'll no doubt see it all makes sense and there's nothing to worry about. You never know, we might get some new tech out of it too."

"Maybe they're all dead on there."

"It's a possibility. In fact, I'd be willing to bet they are. But if that's the case, they're still no threat to us. It's a good battle to go into when your enemy's inanimate."

"Unless what's killed them is still on there."

Another pause, the warrant officer turned to look at his daughter. Deep lines dominated his heavy features as he frowned at her, the darkness of the room only showing Reyes shadows where his eyes were. "Weren't you listening? We can't detect *any* movement on the ship. There's *nothing* on there."

"What if the cause of their death is chemical?"

"What? Like a leak or something?" He shook his head. "We've tested the air and it's perfectly safe. Whatever's caused *The Faradis* to be the way it is, I don't think it poses any threat to us now. Are you still shaken up from the last mission?"

"You're not?"

The warrant officer drew a deep sigh and scratched his thick stubble. The noise of him rubbing his coarse hairs sounded out so loud it damn near echoed in the now nearly empty room. "When you get to my age and have as many years in the Marines as I have, there are very few things that rattle you. I hate that our brothers and sisters died on my watch, but we did the best we could. We need to focus on the ones we saved. *The Faradis* will be a walk in the park compared to what we had to deal with on Q328."

Despite the words coming from his mouth, Reyes heard how his voice cracked. As their leader, he had to be strong.

Many of the Marines didn't know the other side of him. They saw him as a humourless man who always got the job done. Someone they could rely on, but not someone they wanted to be around. Reyes knew him better than that. In the silence that followed, she smirked.

"What?" he said.

Although her smile widened, she batted his question away with a wave of her hand. "Oh, nothing."

"You can't say that now. What are you smiling at?"

"I was just thinking about the chats we used to have at home.

Whenever I had a hard time at school, you'd sit beside me on my bed and tell me everything would be fine. I'd believe you, too."

"And it always was, wasn't it?"

"Mostly, yeah. I love how you tried to fix things for me. To take away my stress and carry the burden yourself."

"Isn't that what a dad should do?"

"Sure, I just wish you'd let it work both ways sometimes. Let me help you once in a while. Soon you'll have to."

"Why?"

"You're no spring chick." Before he could reply, she added with a wry smile, "It won't be long before I'll have to wash out your bedpan, Granddad."

"*Granddad?!*" He reached across and laid a hand against her stomach. "Is there something you're not telling me?"

The humour left her and heat flushed Reyes' cheeks. As much as she wanted to say yes, she rolled her eyes and shook her head, turning away from him. Now wasn't the right time. As she stared at the dark wall beside her, the sting of tears itched her eyes. "Yeah, right," she said, "like *that's* going to happen." She never took the conversation past that point. Just the thought of it made her tremble.

Reyes' dad turned away from her and looked straight ahead at the invisible movie again. After he'd drawn another deep sigh and let it go, he said, "I'll have your back if you choose to come on board *The Faradis*."

"But?"

"I want you to stay here."

"*What?!*"

"I don't want you coming onto this ship with me."

"I thought you said it's going to be a walk in the park?"

"I'm not the kind of man to talk about my feelings, sweetheart, you know that. Especially when I feel scared."

"You're *scared?*"

Clearly still carrying much from their crash on Q328, the WO's eyes glazed as he looked at her. "I still sneak into your room to check you're breathing at night. You know that?"

It took the words from Reyes' mouth.

"That fear that I'll lose you has never left me." He stared down at his clasped hands, his thick knuckles white from how tightly he gripped. "It got worse after Mum died." He looked back up at her, his piercing blue eyes moving from one of hers to the other as if he tried to look into them both at the same time. There was a softness to his voice she didn't often hear, and a tear ran down his cheek. She'd not seen him cry since they'd buried her mum. "I'd just prefer it if you stayed here."

"What aren't you telling me about this ship?"

"Nothing. I've told you everything I know. Besides, if someone told me they had a bad feeling, I'd tell them I dealt with facts, not feelings. I can't pull an easy mission based on a bad feeling." He got to his feet. "It's your choice, sweetheart."

While watching him walk from the room, Reyes' vision blurred. One of these days she'd find the courage to tell him what she needed to. One of these days she'd be brave enough to be able to hear his response.

# CHAPTER 13

Despite the reminder of yet another wasted opportunity to talk to her dad, Reyes had been lifted by the conversation with him and walked into the arena feeling a bit lighter than before. On the *Crimson Destroyer* they were rarely alone in the same place together for long enough to connect. She missed the talks they'd shared when she was a teenager. As guilty as she'd felt for him putting his career on hold after her mum had died, she'd had him to herself back then. For most of the time now she saw him as the warrant officer, and he saw her as another damn rookie. Occasionally they went so long without connecting to one another, she would question if that was all they were.

Then Reyes looked across the murderball court at the Marines gathered there, waiting to go with him on this mission. Could she really stay behind while they went? But it would make her dad happy, and it hadn't been long since they'd returned from Q328.

Two lines of Marines stood in the middle of the large metal hall. A quick count showed her eight in one line and seven in the other—sixteen of them, including her dad at the front. Many of the survivors from Q328 were there: Patel, Simpson, Singh, Holmes, Austin, and Platt. If they had it in them to go, surely she needed to find the resolve too. But the WO hadn't asked them to stay. As she stepped closer, the entire room turned to look at her, including the group of Marines who stood over to one side. The wallflowers who were staying behind.

Before any of the other Marines could speak, her father barked his words out, his loud voice exploding through the cavernous steel room. "What we have here should be more than enough." A look at the group at the side of the hall, he said, "The rest of you need to be ready to get us off *The Faradis* when we need it. Your role back here will be as important as ours on the ship."

Although the warrant officer addressed the group by the wall, many of the Marines lined up in front of him threw momentary glances at Reyes as if expecting her to join them. A dead weight in her legs and with a heavy heart, she trudged over to the group who were staying. It broke her father from his speech for the briefest of moments as he watched her. The slightest of nods, it was about the closest he came to a smile. He then carried on; not that she listened to what he said.

As Reyes scanned the line of Marines bound for *The Faradis*, she made eye contact with a frowning Patel. Although she wanted to explain herself, she didn't. She couldn't derail the briefing to plead to them all. Instead, she dropped her attention to the gunmetal grey floor.

It took a few seconds for Reyes to feel brave enough to look back up again. When she did, she saw Patel had returned his focus to the WO. Most of the others had done the same, and for a moment, Reyes took in his words too.

"This should be a simple mission. I don't expect any problems, but as they say: plan for the worst, hope for the best ..."

Reyes moved her attention away from her dad as she looked down the line of Marines again. The second she'd entered the room, she knew where Chan stood, but she'd avoided looking at her until that moment. They locked stares, holding each other's gaze before the slightest smirk lifted one side of Chan's mouth.

It lit Reyes' fuse, sending a streak of fire through her. Her pulse racing, she bit back her reaction with a tight clamp of her jaw. What the hell did Chan know, and who did she think she was? She hadn't just heard the conversation Reyes had had with her dad. He'd *asked* her to stay back. As a good soldier and a daughter, she had to respect his wishes.

The smug look remained on Chan's bruised face—an expression that would be imprinted in Reyes' mind for the rest of her days. Every time she closed her eyes, she'd see that snide little grin. It would remind her of the time she didn't have the stones to board *The Faradis*. The time the great hero from Q328 lost her nerve. Even though that wasn't the case, Chan wouldn't believe her, and she'd never be able to persuade her otherwise. Reyes planned to spend most of her adult life as a Marine. Chan didn't look to be going anywhere either. Every new recruit would hear about how Reyes lost her nerve on one of the easiest missions in their squad's history. Maybe she'd also remind her that it was okay to be scared. Everyone got scared—even Marines. Of course, Chan never got scared, but Reyes shouldn't compare herself to Chan. That would only make her miserable.

The words lurched from Reyes as an involuntary reaction, her voice cutting off the warrant officer mid-sentence and taking the attention of the entire room. "I'm coming!"

Silence fell over the large metal arena. Thirty plus Marines all stared at her like she'd lost her mind. None of them spoke.

Chan broke the silence with a snigger. "All right, love, I know we all like the tension before a mission"—she tapped her head and spoke in a fake whisper—"but maybe you should know that sharing isn't *always* caring."

As much as she wanted to hit back at her, Reyes couldn't defend her outburst. Her cheeks on fire, she listened to several of the other Marines laugh at Chan's joke while she looked at her dad, cleared her throat, and spoke with a warble in her voice, much quieter than her outburst of moments ago. "I'm coming on the mission."

The slightest narrowing around the WO's eyes, he looked from his daughter to the lined-up Marines and back to his daughter. As much as she knew he wanted to say no, he showed no other outward sign of his disappointment. Instead, he nodded in the direction of the lined-up Marines and said, "Get over here, then."

Reyes moved in behind Julius, who stood at the back of the shorter line. Julius always stood at the back. The tallest of all the Marines, she served as a perfect shield for Reyes to hide behind.

Julius turned around and looked down at her with raised eyebrows. "You sure you want to stand there?"

Reyes nodded.

"You won't be able to see."

In a voice so quiet only Julius could hear, Reyes said, "That's fine." She then looked at the floor as if she could direct her boiling shame into the cold metal at her feet. How could she have even considered not going? On Q328 she saw there wasn't much she could have done to save the Marines who perished, but if the mission on *The Faradis* turned south and she'd stayed back on the *Crimson Destroyer*, she wouldn't be able to live with herself.

Instead of the expected warrant officer's voice, Reyes heard Chan's. "Are you sure she's going to be okay coming with us, WO? I don't want to overstep the mark, but she seems a bit emotional right now. I wonder if that last mission was too much for her. Maybe she needs more time to process it. I wouldn't want to tell you your job, but I want to speak to the safety of the mission to make sure we don't take someone who's likely to be a liability with us. I just—"

Where Reyes expected her father's voice for a second time,

Patel shouted at Chan instead, his shrieking tone taking flight in the large space. "Wind your neck in, soldier! You have *no* idea what Reyes did to get us out of that cove. You keep going for her like you are and I'm sure I'm not the only one who'll ask the WO to leave *you* behind instead. I'd take Reyes over you any day of the week."

Several Marines made noises that backed up Patel's comments.

Although Reyes couldn't see them from behind Julius, she heard Chan draw a breath to respond, but the warrant officer cut her off. "If you two have finished bitching at one another, I'd like to talk about the mission."

Silence.

Reyes heard the hurt in her dad's voice. What hadn't he told her about *The Faradis*? Did he know something, or was it just a bad feeling like he'd said?

"Have you finished?"

Silence.

"Good. So the plan is to board *The Faradis*. There are seventeen of us, which should be plenty. I anticipate we'll find the crew. My guess is they'll all be expired, but I'm hoping their corpses will offer some insight as to how they got into their current situation. We know the air's not toxic because we've tested it, and we know there's nothing alive on board because we've scanned for heat signatures. So if something has poisoned or slaughtered them, it's not there anymore. I'm not expecting this to turn into a gunfight, because there's nothing on board to fight. Still, I want you to arm up, suit up, and ..."

In the pause, Reyes leaned around Julius' wide frame to see the WO staring straight at Chan. "Grow up," he said. She watched her dad pinch and then massage the top of his nose as if he had a headache. When he spoke again, resignation weighted his tone. "There's no evidence to show we have anything to worry about on this ship, but that doesn't mean you shouldn't all bring your A game."

For the last few minutes Reyes had boiled with shame. Sweat itched around her collar and beneath her armpits. But after hearing her dad's final words and thinking about his bad feeling, her blood turned cold. What were they about to embark on?

# CHAPTER 14

To be back in the armoury so soon after Q328 quickened Reyes' heartbeat, her throat tightening. Had she taken on this mission too soon? Was that why her dad had told her to remain on the *Crimson Destroyer*? Maybe he didn't feel any apprehension about *The Faradis*.

Fighting against her own body, Reyes pulled in a deep breath, her chest expanding. She had to go on this mission. What had happened on Q328 kept her awake at night, but she didn't dream of the monsters when she fell into fitful bursts of sleep. She dreamed about the corpses of those she cared for: her brothers and sisters torn apart in the sandy cove while she watched on from behind a locked door. In her dreams she banged against the glass. She screamed their names, and when she finally woke from the nightmares, she was always drenched in sweat and they were always still dead. The heat of the planet remained inside her like a fever. Maybe she could make good on her failings by boarding *The Faradis* with the others. Maybe she'd sleep better when they returned. When she looked up and made eye contact with Chan, she saw the small Marine narrow her blackened eyes. The swelling around them already looked worse. Reason number two for going on the mission. If she didn't, Chan wouldn't ever let her forget it.

The armoury had originally been designed as a chapel until the shipbuilders sold the *Crimson Destroyer*—which wasn't the name they'd given it—to the Marines. The ceiling stretched higher than the one in the murderball arena, giving wings to every noise made by the Marines: the clicks of harnesses and armour; the low murmur of conversation; coughs—some nervous, some not. They all soared in the empty space above them. A long rectangular room, it had been left plain. No doubt the builders were waiting for a buyer before they customised it with the garish display of whichever religion they preferred. The room lifted at one end, providing a raised platform for a preacher to deliver his wisdom to his congregation. The army, however, had zero tolerance for any outward displays of religion. They believed it to be personal, and while they respected a Marine's right to have whatever faith they chose, they expected them to keep it to themselves. The Marines' gods were semi-automatic and had a blast radius.

The floor had tracks running through it, designed for pews to slot into, but rows of shelves slid in just as easily. The place now looked more like a library than a chapel; however, instead of books, the shelves were home to blasters, grenades, and armour.

When Reyes tugged on the straps of her flak vest before pressing the clip shut, she exhaled to feel the press of her stomach against it. She looked at the others standing close to her. They were the survivors from Q328: Patel, Austin, Platt, Simpson, Singh, and Holmes. Their shared experience had bonded them tighter to one another. They'd gained a level of trust that could only be earned.

Reyes met Patel's eyes when she looked at him. He appeared to be waiting for her to glance his way. "The WO seemed a little bit off?" he said, lifting his voice on the last word of his statement, turning it into a question.

At first Reyes didn't respond. The conversation in the briefing room had been private. Besides, who wanted to know their commanding officer had a bad feeling about a mission just before they embarked on it? "I think the last mission shook us all up. It's a bit much to have to go out again so soon."

Several of the others nodded, the click of harnesses tightening as they put on their armour.

Singh spoke this time. "But I've never seen him look apprehensive before."

"Do you think we're all going to die on this mission?" A slight smile lifted Austin's lips. Nearly a foot taller than Singh, he loomed over her naturally. Whenever he stood next to her, he played on the fact. Dropping his voice low, he peered down on her. "The shadows might attack us the second we get on board."

After tutting at him, Singh shook her head and slapped her palm against his chest, driving him back a couple of steps. "Do you always need to be such a dick?"

Reyes smiled and shook her head as she watched Austin blow a kiss at Singh, who replied with a raised middle finger.

Despite the banter, they were now all looking at Reyes again. She clearly hadn't given them a satisfactory answer to Patel's question. She knew the warrant officer better than any of them and had had a private conversation with him only minutes before the briefing; she must have information he hadn't given the rest of the team. But the more she said about it, the easier they'd be able to see her lie. She shrugged. "I suppose all we can do is arm up and keep our wits." A rack of blasters close by, she turned to them and took two semi-automatic handguns.

Just before Reyes holstered the blasters, a hand came from behind her and wrapped a strong grip around one of them. Not that she needed to turn around to see who the hand belonged to. Chan whispered in her ear, "Two's a bit greedy, isn't it? Especially as it's the last two left."

The attention of the others on her, Reyes rolled her eyes before she looked at Chan. "Do you really have to fight me for *everything?* This has been going on for two years now. What's your problem?"

"I'm not the one with the problem, dear. You are. *You're* the fake, not me."

"You've said that before. What the hell are you talking about?" When Chan didn't reply, Reyes said, "There are plenty of other weapons here. Go and find something else."

But Chan didn't let go. Instead, she tugged on the blaster again. "What if only this gun will do? Come on, Reyes, don't be so selfish. You have *two*, after all. We're all in this together, you know?" Before Reyes could reply, she added, "Besides, you've beaten our deadliest opponent yet with nothing but a torch to light your way, so what do *you* need blasters for? You've damn near got superpowers." A facetious smile, the effect losing its impact because of her two black eyes, she tugged on the gun again.

Although Reyes ground her jaw and refused to yield to Chan, she didn't respond.

"Stop being a muppet, Chan," Patel said.

Where her face had been lit up to be provoking Reyes, Chan turned to Patel with her top lip raised in a snarl. "Watch your mouth, Marine."

"What?" Patel balled his fists. "Who do you think you are?"

"I'm not pulling rank. I'm just warning you to keep out. This is between me and daddy's girl."

Reyes scanned her friends to see all of them twitching as if they were about to grab their weapons. They didn't need to be falling out before they went on that cursed ship. Also, it didn't matter how much Chan deserved it, the warrant officer would come down hard on her just for retaliating. He'd treat her like she'd started it. He wouldn't want to hear anything to the contrary. Besides, whatever her dad felt worried about, it would be a lot worse if they went on *The Faradis* with a division in the ranks. She let go of the blaster.

When it came free, Chan stared at it for a second. The tight wind of her shoulders loosened. Before she could say anything, Reyes handed her the other one. "I took both of these because I know they're a deadly combination. I want you to have them. It's more important to me that you go onto *The Faradis* happy. I can use something else and would hate to disadvantage you for no reason."

Although Reyes kept her focus on Chan, she couldn't help but notice the smirks on her friends' faces all around them.

Chan took both guns and slowly turned to look at the others. The same snarl on her face, she tutted, shook her head, and walked away.

Before Chan had gone from earshot, Patel said, "What's *her* problem?"

But Reyes didn't reply. As much as Patel wanted to goad Chan and sought a collaborator, if things did go south on *The Faradis*, Chan would be a handy ally. Besides, she'd already won; she didn't need to rub it in.

# CHAPTER 15

S eventeen Marines, including the WO, they were now armed and ready to go, standing in front of the double doors leading to the now pressurised and airlocked corridor connecting them to *The Faradis* like an umbilical cord. The grizzled veteran stood in front of them again. He clasped his hands while he paced back and forth. This time, Reyes stood closer to the front, Julius returning to her natural position at the end of the line.

"You all have mics and earpieces in your helmets," the warrant officer said. "Now, I'm not planning on using them, because I want us to stay together, but in case anything should happen, I want everyone to switch theirs on now. Our intel tells me everything will be fine. We've scanned *The Faradis* and can't see any signs of movement. We know we can breathe on there. I'm not stoked that I only have a team of rookies with me, but many of you have been to hell and survived it already. I expect you to step up and help the others if they need it."

Although Chan didn't look around, Reyes saw her shake her head at his comment. Unfortunately for Chan, he saw it too.

"Do you have a problem, Marine?"

An almost instant reply, Chan slammed her boot down in a

hard stamp as if driving her frustration away. "No, WO, sir. Sorry, sir." The silence between the two turned the air thick. The warrant officer finally broke it. "There seems little point in saying much else other than let's make this quick. Get in, work out why the ship's abandoned, and then get back in time for lunch."

In the silence that responded to him, Reyes looked around, her eyes landing on Julius. She noticed the large Marine had a tight grip on her gun. As much as she looked like she tried to fight the shake running through her hands, she failed miserably. It could be because she hadn't been on a mission yet. The majority of them carried that burden. It could also be the clear apprehension in the WO's voice. Although he'd not said it outright, his speech shared his worry with the rest of them. Hopefully it would have the positive effect of keeping everyone sharp rather than leeching their confidence and turning them into a liability. A more experienced head in the group, she'd made the correct choice to come with them. They might need her and the other survivors from Q328.

Before Reyes could think on it any further, the *whoosh* of the doors to the airlocked corridor opened. The warrant officer didn't look back or speak again. Instead, he waited for the doors to fully part before he stepped into the corridor. The slamming down of his first step hit the floor as a loud *boom* in the tight space. The squad followed him in. Despite all of them marching forward, Reyes felt the same reluctance in them that tugged on her own tired muscles.

The WO reached the next set of doors first, Reyes now directly behind him. He turned to watch the rest of the Marines. After the *whoosh* signalling the first set of doors closing, he slammed a hard fist against the button to open the ones leading onto the alien ship.

Another *whoosh* and the blood-red glow of *The Faradis*' emergency lighting flooded into the small space. Even the warrant officer paused for a second, and Reyes felt the tension around her wind that little bit tighter, her own shoulders aching. Maybe they should go back. Find another way to explore the ship. Or just let it pass. When he stepped forward, her stomach lurched. Too late to back out now.

The second Reyes entered the ship, she gasped. The design looked like nothing she'd seen before. Where she'd been used to almost black steel on the *Crimson Destroyer*, *The Faradis* took it to a whole new level. Obsidian-like, the black metal had a glossy glow to it that made it look wet. Where she had been used to a standard design made up of right angles, straight walls, and levelled floors, she saw none of that here. *The Faradis* had an organic look to it. Almost as if it had been grown rather than built.

The corridor stretched away from them like a tunnel that had been burrowed instead of constructed. Round walls as if a large worm had eaten its way through, the metal on every surface was uneven like the bark of a tree or the knotting of varicose veins. Where the *Crimson Destroyer* had lights dotted along the ceiling, *The Faradis* had lights wherever they could fit them. As many above their head as by their feet or in the wall on either side of them, each one deepened the ominous crimson glow.

When Reyes drew a deep breath to try to still her quickened pulse, she inhaled the reek of oil, the sharp tang of it catching in the back of her throat so she could almost taste it. It didn't smell like the used oil of a working engine. It had a more organic aroma to it, like it had been harvested from crops or animals.

Her attention captured by the strange ship, when Reyes finally looked at the others, she saw they were all as mesmerised, including her father. And why wouldn't they be? It looked like they'd entered a different dimension. One altogether darker than the one they were leaving; no wonder the warrant officer couldn't hide his apprehension from his tone when he'd briefed them.

It took for him to set off again before any of the others moved. The only sound in the huge ship came from their cautious steps against the uneven floor. Every time Reyes put a foot down, it turned and twisted. How would she run through the place if she needed to? What kind of creatures had lived on board to make such a surface preferable? Although, the scans had shown the place to be abandoned, so it didn't matter what had lived here before. It certainly looked and sounded unoccupied. Maybe she should take solace from the silence rather than create beings that weren't there.

Despite the red lighting stretching away from them down the corridor, Reyes couldn't see far enough to know where it ended. But from her position close to the front of the pack, she did see the closed double doors up ahead on the right.

At the doors, the WO stopped for a second before pointing at Reyes, Patel, Singh, and Austin. "You four, keep watch down that corridor while we open these doors."

Reyes, Patel, Singh, and Austin held their ground while the warrant officer pressed the button next to the double doors. A *whoosh* sounded out as they opened. The others went through first. They all had their weapons raised, hoping for the best but planning for the worst.

The last to enter the room, Reyes followed the others in. Much like the corridor, the large dining hall looked like it had been grown rather than constructed. A complex twist of black steel, the ceiling sat as a dome over the wide space. The tables and chairs looked to have sprouted from the floor rather than been placed there.

Although Reyes stepped close to one of the tables, she stood as silent as the rest of them and looked at the wide eyes and open mouths around her. From their expressions, it seemed clear that none of them had seen anything like it before.

The bark of the WO's gruff voice made Reyes' heart kick, and she clapped a hand to her chest. Chan threw a sharp scowl of disdain at her. "It looks like whatever happened to the crew," he said, "it happened quickly enough to catch them unawares."

Not food she recognised, Reyes looked at the tables. Even the seating positions appeared to be set up for a species very different to human. She moved closer to one of the plates with food still on it and reached out to touch it. The second her fingertips made contact, she froze. It took a few attempts to find the words. "Um, WO?"

He and the rest of the squad turned to look at her. "I …" Her hand shook as she continued to touch the food. "I think whatever crew they had on this ship was here until only very recently."

"What makes you say that?"

Reyes pulled in a warm and arid gulp before she said, "This food is still hot."

# CHAPTER 16

I nstead of replying to Reyes, the WO picked up a mug and held it in front of his face as if getting a closer look would help him ascertain the temperature of the liquid. Even from where she stood several metres away, Reyes saw the steam rising from it. Despite the high and intricate domed ceiling above them, she hunched as she felt like the room was closing down on her. Maybe they should have listened to her dad's bad feeling in the first place.

From the quick glance she threw around the room, Reyes saw all the Marines were watching the warrant officer as he placed the mug back down on the table, opening and closing his hand because he'd clearly held onto the hot vessel for too long. He then pulled his tablet from his pocket. After several taps against the screen, he let go of a long and deflating sigh. "This entire room is above the engine." The echo of his voice seemed more pronounced than it had a few seconds ago. The silence it broke, more complete.

When no one replied, he elaborated. "The heat coming from the ship's engine masked the heat of this food because it's not got a pulse." With a look down at some of the strange meats on display, he added, "At least, I don't think any of this lot has a pulse. We missed it on the scan—not that I think it matters. It only tells us what we now know anyway: there's hot food in this room. But I'm still confident there are no living beings."

Maybe Reyes spoke out of turn, but she still asked him, "Are there any more heat sources on the ship that we need to be aware of?"

The WO wore his usual thick scowl as he looked at her and then back down at his tablet. He shook his head. "Not according to this, there isn't."

The rest of the Marines watched the conversation between Reyes and her dad like spectators at a tennis match. An awareness of them in her peripheral vision, she continued to focus on the warrant officer. "Then where have they gone? How can an entire crew just disappear?"

Reyes saw several of the Marines look around them, the paranoia palpable in the large and intricate hall. The deep crimson glow of the place created many shadows, shadows that could hide many secrets.

This time, Chan spoke. "Maybe they passed through the Corinthian's Diamond?"

"The *what?*" Patel said, unable to hide his disdain for her. And she'd earned it. She'd been more of an arsehole than usual when they were in the armoury. She could end up being a liability on this mission if she kept it up.

A slight twist to her bruised face, Chan locked her jaw tight as if biting back her words. She drew a deep inhale through her nose and remained fixed on Patel as she let the air out through her mouth. She then said, "The Corinthian's Diamond." She paused for a second as if she needed another moment to keep her cool. "It's a region near Bulbulai 7. A lot of weird shit happens there. Entire fleets are rumoured to have gone missing without a trace."

The WO's gruff voice made them all jump when he said,

"This situation is strange enough without us using ghost stories as a basis for trying to understand it. You just said it yourself, Chan: they're *rumours.* Unless anyone has something worth saying— and preferably something that's rooted in rational thought—then I don't want to hear it. There's nothing to be gained from creating enemies that don't exist. We don't want to defeat ourselves with our own paranoia before we've even started. You got that?"

None of the Marines answered, so he said, "*Chan!* I said have you got that?"

A little bit more successful at reining it in with the WO than she had been with Patel, Chan showed no outward sign of rage as she looked at the dark and twisted metal floor and nodded. "Yes, sir. Sorry. It was a ridiculous idea."

The WO had just confirmed to Reyes why he hadn't acted on his bad feeling. He'd said it to keep her off *The Faradis*, but since she'd made her decision to come anyway, he refused to let paranoia be their enemy. A curse of the human condition, they could keep it at bay with a strong will. Failing that, they needed to keep it to themselves rather than let it spread like witches' fire. They had no evidence for bad feelings or hunches. They couldn't base their decisions on them.

A slightly calmer voice than a few seconds ago, the warrant officer nodded. "I understand everyone's a bit jumpy. This is beyond weird, but that doesn't mean it's supernatural. We need to stick together, do a sweep of this ship, work out what's going on, and then take action. I'll listen to theories, but let's not spook each other unnecessarily, okay?"

Before anyone could reply, a deep *clunk* ran through the vessel. So heavy, Reyes felt it through the soles of her boots and thrust her arms out to the sides as if to brace herself for a fall.

In light of the WO's recent outburst, none of the Marines commented on the noise, but every one of them stood with more tension in their frame.

The sound of radio static pierced the silence. Reyes watched her father hold his tablet up as a tinny and high-pitched voice called through the small speakers. "WO, this is the *Crimson Destroyer*. Can you please tell us why you've disconnected the two vessels? Over."

Radio protocol out of the window, the warrant officer lifted his tablet to his mouth. "We haven't."

Before he could say anything else, the floor beneath Reyes' feet shook and rumbled. She looked around the room at the exits on either side for some clue as to what was happening. It showed her nothing other than two closed sets of double doors.

"Sir, why are you starting the engines on *The Faradis*?"

With a spike in his voice and panic Reyes had never heard in his tone before, he said, "We're *not*. You have to do something. Use the *Crimson Destroyer* to stop it getting away."

"I'm not sure I can. We have no power to override their controls from here, sir. Not now we're disconnected."

The vibration through the floor grew stronger, the whir of the engines beneath them louder.

The Marine on the *Crimson Destroyer* spoke again, his words gathering in pitch and momentum. "WO, *The Faradis* is preparing to make the jump to hyperspace. There's nothing we can do to stop it."

Without another word, the warrant officer shoved his way past the Marines as he headed back in the direction of the doors they'd just entered through. As the last in, it allowed Reyes to follow directly behind the heavy and awkward gait of her old man. They moved down the organic and dimly lit corridor. All the while, the sound of the engines grew louder, swelling with the charging power of it getting ready to make the jump.

The WO reached the end of the corridor, Reyes directly behind him. With just about enough room for her and her dad to see out of the small window in the door, she looked across the dark gap of space between them and the *Crimson Destroyer*. Already fifty metres at least, she saw the face of Archer watching them through the window on his side. Eyes wide, he stared across the silent space between them.

"What are we going to do?" Reyes said.

Before her dad could answer, the sound of the engine reached its crescendo and *The Faradis* accelerated away. The *Crimson Destroyer* vanished from sight as they made the jump into hyperspace.

# CHAPTER 17

R eyes stood beside her dad as they both stared out into space where the *Crimson Destroyer* had been only a few seconds earlier. The rest of the Marines had remained in the dining hall, and maybe Reyes should have too. "Where are we?"

He pulled his tablet from his pocket and flicked it on. The glow from the backlit screen threw shadows across his heavyset face. When he didn't answer her immediately, Reyes' stomach turned backflips. The longer he spent staring down at the illumi-nated device—his frown deepening with every passing second—the less she wanted to know where they'd ended up.

"I've got no idea," he finally said. "I don't have the star systems for this area downloaded on the tablet, and for some reason I can't contact any local satellites."

"But there are satellites everywhere."

"I don't think it's missing satellites we have to worry about. I think they're still there."

"But *The Faradis* is blocking our connection to them?"

"That's my guess."

As much as Reyes wanted to remain calm, she could hear her

own panic as quickened breaths in the confined space. "So we can't contact the *Crimson Destroyer*?"

"I told you not to come, didn't I? You should be on the *Crimson Destroyer* still."

A glance into the red glow of the long corridor behind her, Reyes saw they were still alone. "What good would that have done?"

"It would have given me someone I trust with my life tracking me down." Before Reyes could reply, he said, "We need to go back to the dining hall and talk to the others. We're up shit creek. They need to know that, and we need to come up with a plan to get back to our mothership."

Reyes didn't try to talk to him, and he didn't look like he wanted her to as they walked back to the dining hall. When they entered the domed metal room, she saw many of the Marines had sat down at the twisted tables, perching themselves on the awkward stools. Every pair of eyes fixed on them.

"We've lost contact with the *Crimson Destroyer*," the warrant officer announced.

His words fell dead in the large room, and Reyes saw the blood drain from many faces, even beneath the crimson lights.

"For some reason," he continued, "*The Faradis* has made the jump to hyperspace. I don't know where it's taken us." The only sound came from the stamp of his heavy boots as he walked over to Julius and gave her his tablet. "I think the ship's blocking us from contacting any local satellites. Can you see if you can find a way around it? We need to get a distress signal off this ship to the *Crimson Destroyer* ASAP."

"So what shall we do?" Chan said.

The WO shrugged. "That's what we need to work out."

"What? You don't have a plan?"

"Remember your place, Marine. And of course I don't have a plan. Do you seriously think I would have gotten on board if I'd have known it was going to take us light-years away from our mothership? The plan was to get on here, find out why it had no crew, and then get off. That plan's now changed."

"We're screwed."

This time Reyes responded. "Not helpful, Chan. Unless you've got something constructive to say, I suggest you keep your mouth shut."

The same tight clench to her jaw, Chan's swollen eyes narrowed, but she didn't reply.

Because of the silence, Reyes looked back at the WO, slightly startled to find him staring at her. "You'd do well to take your own advice," he said.

Reyes' cheeks burned and she dropped her attention to the floor. Although her dad went extra hard on her because he had to, she'd earned that. She had no right to talk to anyone in that way. A rookie should know their place.

Julius—who'd been busying herself with the tablet since it had been handed to her—stood up, drawing the room's attention. It took some of the focus off Reyes, the heat in her face cooling as she too watched the tall Marine walk over to one of the dark walls. After she'd tapped the tablet's screen, she then held it up to project an image in front of her. "I've not managed to connect to any satellites, but I have managed to pull this from the ship's local network. These are the schematics for *The Faradis*. I don't think I can go any deeper into their systems than this, at least, not with this tablet."

Because the warrant officer had shown them what *The Faradis* looked like from the outside when he briefed them, the shape laid out on the schematic looked familiar.

Julius pressed against the tablet's screen again, a small white dot appearing on the projected image to show what she pointed at. "We entered the main section of the ship here, and this is where we are now." They were in the first of a series of rooms down the centre of the larger middle section. It looked like a corridor ran down either side, giving access to all the rooms from both ends.

Like they'd seen from the outside, *The Faradis* was made up of what looked to be three large rockets. Resembling silos lying flat, the main one in the middle and the two smaller ones were connected on either side of it. Boosters were at the end of either of the small rockets. The external design looked like something a child would dream up. The dark organic twist of the inside looked like something birthed in the bowels of hell.

The white light showed how the main body of the ship had six rooms down the centre of it. "We're in the dining hall," Julius said. "The next room along is the control room. Then the library. Then the dry food stores. A briefing room. And finally a sports hall. I can only guess their dorms are in the smaller sections along with showers, fuel storage, and most importantly, the …" She paused as if nervous to say it.

"The what?" the WO said.

A sigh, Julius continued to focus on the schematic in front of her. "The escape pods."

"And we can't see anything of what's in the other two sections?" he asked.

A shake of her head, Julius winced. "It looks like we're locked in this middle section. Not only are we unable to get to the two smaller segments, but I can't see what's in them either, for some reason."

Singh stood up, and the rest of the room looked at her. "It seems to me that we need to search this section of the ship. If we can find a way to access the rest of it, we might be able to get off here. I mean, there's still no sign of any other living beings, so maybe the jump into hyperspace was a malfunction." She winced when she said, "Right?"

Although she shrugged and nodded, Julius didn't look

convinced. "We certainly haven't seen any evidence of any other living beings on here."

Because Julius didn't offer anything else, the room turned and looked at the warrant officer, who nodded his approval. "I agree with Singh. Unless someone has a better idea?"

After looking at the Marines around him, he clapped his hands together as if to inspire them to act. "Right. Time to get a plan into place. We search this section from end to end and top to bottom. If we do that, we're bound to find some way off this godforsaken vessel."

"I think we should split up, too," Reyes said. "The quicker we search this thing, the better. I don't know about anyone else, but I want to get off here as soon as is humanly possible."

A slight narrowing of his eyes, the WO appeared not to like the idea at first. But he didn't argue with her and, after a few seconds, nodded. "Good idea." He then went on to say, "I wish I could give us a plan beyond that, but I don't know what we're going to find. None of us do. Following Singh's suggestion is better than waiting here doing nothing."

# CHAPTER 18

L ike a sports teacher dividing the class, the warrant officer went through the pack of Marines and split them into two teams: eight on one side, nine on the other. When he put Reyes and Chan together, Reyes said, "Are you sure?"

As curt and gruff as ever, her dad scowled. "Don't question me, rookie. Unless you want to lead this mission? Q328 looks like it's gone to your head. You made a lucky guess about those creatures; don't think of it as any more than that."

Reyes took the berating. He had to be harder on her. Besides, she'd earned it. Again. Now he'd made his decision on what they were doing next, she had no right to question it. He only wanted input when he expressly asked for it. To avoid his strong glare, she looked away from him, making eye contact with Chan. The small Marine stared straight back with dead eyes.

"You," the WO said to Reyes' group. He then pointed at the double doors on the far side of the dining hall, the ones that led to the corridor they hadn't yet walked down. "You go out there."

They set off, following Reyes to the other side of the room. Before they got to the doors, the WO shouted across the high-ceilinged space, "Reyes, you lead that team. Chan, you respect that or we'll send you out in an airlock. I don't need your ego jeopardising this mission."

"My ego would never jeopardise a mission, *sir*. Any problem I have with Reyes won't be detrimental to my professionalism."

Although Chan sounded almost convincing, Reyes had had two years of her bullshit and didn't feel ready to trust her just yet.

The warrant officer continued. "We're going to move down the two corridors, searching them as we make our way to the next room, where the comms are. Hopefully we can get a signal out to the *Crimson Destroyer* and work out what's going on with the rest of this ship. Any questions?"

Reyes watched those around her to see if they'd respond. When they didn't, she paired her team up. Patel, Singh, and Austin had been put with her. She gave each of them a partner, and she took Chan. No way could she drop that firecracker on anyone else. Besides, she needed to keep her in line.

As she watched her dad lead his team out through the doors on the opposite side of the hall, Reyes turned to those with her. "We go down the corridor two at a time. Chan and I will lead. I want Patel and Lombardo at the back; are you two okay with that?"

Both Patel and Lombardo nodded.

"The scanners suggest this ship's empty, but we need to keep our wits. Something's not right on here, so stay vigilant. Plan for the worst …" She left her words hanging. They'd said it so many times her team could fill in the blanks. Also, she didn't have much hope things would turn out for the best. Better to not say it than to lie. The conversation she'd had with her dad in the briefing room had stayed with her. His bad feeling now ran through her veins.

All the while she spoke, Reyes felt the fierce burn of Chan's focus directed at her. "Do you have something you need to say before we go into this? I know you're a good soldier. I need you focusing on keeping us alive, not on your petty grudge."

"*Petty?*"

"Look, whatever it is, you haven't told me for the past two years, and I don't care to know now. All that matters is whether I can trust you or not."

The small Chan straightened her back, standing that little bit taller than before. "Did you not just listen to what I said? Do you seriously think I'll screw up a mission because I hate you?"

"She's not trying to argue with you, Chan," Lombardo said. "Besides, you're not doing a good job of proving we can trust you." The rest of the team appeared to back her up, all of them staring hostility at Chan.

Reyes looked across the dark dining hall to see the doors close behind the WO and his team as the last of them walked out of the room. The sound of her dad's voice came through the radio in her helmet. "You don't need a mother's meeting, Reyes. Get moving."

"Roger that, sir." Reyes spoke while watching Chan to see the same scowl she'd grown used to. Her blaster raised to her shoulder, she flicked on the torch at the end of it and led her team out into the dark corridor. A momentary flashback from their night-time escape on Q328 slammed into her mind. She saw one of the rock creatures growl at her and flinched. It nearly halted her progress. A quick shake of her head to banish the memory, she pushed forward. As long as she kept moving, her trauma wouldn't catch up to her. She didn't need to be dealing with it right now.

The corridor had the same organic twist of metal as the first one they'd walked down. It looked as if the tunnel had been burrowed rather than engineered. The same lighting ran down it, red glows punching from seemingly random points. Everywhere the crimson bulbs tried to illuminate the way, they lost their battle to the shadows. The same ghostly silence lurked in the darkness up ahead.

The glow of more torches from behind her, the white beams bouncing off the black obsidian-like shine of their surroundings, Reyes edged slowly towards the next set of doors farther down. Only a ten-metre walk at the most, she arrived at them without incident. Despite being at the entrance to the control room, she continued to stare down the corridor into the darkness, her pulse fast and her throat dry.

Patel's voice came at her from the back. "We're all here, Reyes."

Reyes pressed the microphone button on the side of her helmet. "WO, we're ready when you are."

"Good," his gruff voice came back. "Let's go in, in three … two … one …"

On *one,* Reyes slammed her palm against the button to open the door. The *crack* of it ran both ways down the dark tunnel. Despite the card reader next to it, it opened without the need for any extra security.

A titan of a creature unlike any Reyes had seen before stood in the centre of the room. Bipedal, it had six arms, white eyes the size of tank tyres, and thick red skin. Its deep roar shook the ground, and the walls hummed with the vibration of it. Over fifteen feet tall, it had to hunch because its head nearly touched the ceiling.

When a shot ran over Reyes' shoulder from one of her team behind, she pointed at its head. "Shoot up. The other team are opposite us."

While unloading into the creature's face, Reyes watched the thing turn and look down at her. The horns of a ram spiralled from either side of its ugly and angular head. Eyes of fire, it opened its wide black mouth. What looked to be embers burned in its throat as it inhaled. It gave off the charred reek of a smelting furnace.

Reyes flinched away, expecting to be smothered in fire, but the hot rush didn't come. Instead, a green laser blast burst from the beast's right leg.

Reyes didn't react quickly enough. Were it not for Chan shoving her aside—knocking her to the hard metal ground—the green blast that sailed past her would have scored a direct hit. Instead, she watched the shot strike Lombardo, knocking the Marine down with a burst of blood. Reyes and Chan stared at one another for the briefest of seconds, both of them panting, both of them wide-eyed.

Before Reyes could say anything else, another shot came through the creature. She dodged it again and watched sparks explode from the wall behind her when it hit. While pressing the microphone button on the side of her helmet, she shouted, "Stop firing. The shots are going straight through it."

Reyes' team had already stopped shooting, and after her warning, the WO's team did the same. The creature in the centre of the room looked from side to side and roared again. But they held their nerve and none of them fired on it.

Julius' voice then came through the headsets. "It's a projection. The ship's in defence mode. It's a poor attempt at scaring would-be attackers away. That creature's not real. It can't do us any harm."

While looking down at the dead Lombardo, a seared hole through the centre of her face, Reyes said, "It already has. Lombardo's down."

"Down?" The warrant officer's voice replied this time.

"Dead," Reyes said. She shook her head as she stared at her friend. "She took a shot to the face."

# CHAPTER 19

The creature that had looked so intimidating just moments ago shimmered and then vanished. It revealed the WO on the other side of the room as he walked towards Reyes and her team. The tight lock of his thick jaw looked like he could chew through steel. A heavy frown, he fixed on his daughter, moving with the same awkward limp from a body that carried too many injuries.

When he got to about a metre away from them, his eyes lingered on Reyes for a second longer than felt natural. His stare might have appeared impassive to most, but it spoke volumes to her; she shouldn't have come on this mission. He then dropped his attention to the fallen Lombardo and released a hard sigh. "What a damn waste."

Despite the years her father had spent in the job, Reyes saw how hard he took the loss of every single Marine. If anything, as she'd watched him get older, she would have said he felt them more deeply. Another life lost to a never-ending war born from so many species and planets trying to share the same galaxy. A futile battle, the only quantifiable marker came from the number of headstones in the countless cemeteries. A glaze of tears covered his eyes as he continued to look down at the dead Marine before he pointed over to a shadowy corner. "Put her over there. We're taking her body back with us when we get off this damn ship."

Patel and Chan bent down to pick up her body.

Reyes watched Patel lift Lombardo's shoulders and turn his head to the side so he didn't have to look at the hole seared through her face. She turned back to her father. People died; she needed to deal with it. It didn't mean Lombardo's passing didn't matter, but it didn't matter more than those who were still alive. She had to shelve her hurt for now. She cleared her throat. "I've never seen anything like that monster before. Is it something that exists in real life or a fantasy created to ward off strangers?"

The WO's eyes were still glazed. For a second, he didn't speak, breathing through his nose because of the strong clench of his teeth. He then moved so close to Reyes she could smell the sweat on his skin and feel his breath in her ear. When he spoke, he kept his voice low so only she could hear it. "You wouldn't be here if you'd listened to me."

"It wasn't my fault Lombardo got shot. I would have gladly taken the hit in her place. I'd take the hit for any Marine here."

A slight crack in his voice as his composure wavered. "That's the problem. If you'd have just listened to me, you'd be on the *Crimson Destroyer* away from this bullshit." Although Reyes wanted to respond, he pulled away from her and barked across the room, "Julius, get to the computer and see what you can do."

Now the projection had gone, Reyes looked around the space. It stretched as wide as the dining hall from door to door. From the look of the schematic Julius had shown them, all the rooms were the same width. The ceiling stood as high as the apex of the dome in the canteen. However, the control room looked like an altogether more functional space. Rectangular in shape, but the surface of the shiny obsidian-like metal still had the same erratic layering and twist to it.

As Reyes looked up at the ceiling again—the entire room cast in the red glow of emergency lighting—a more apt comparison for the metal's aesthetic hit her. Not so much roots or veins, it resembled seriously damaged skin—skin that had been melted and grafted back together again. Stretched lines of livid flesh from where it had healed in an attempt to reconnect and reclaim its original form. Instead of turning the wound into nothing but a memory, it offered a horrific approximation of what the skin had once been, an ugly reminder of the searing trauma. *The Faradis* might have been made from a metal of sorts, but the longer she spent on the cursed ship, the more it made her think of a failed genetic experiment. Like something a modern-day Dr. Frankenstein would dream up in a dark lab on a remote planet free from codes of conduct and regulation. The kind of place where they stitched moonjab rodents together, arse to mouth, just because they wanted to observe their reaction.

When Reyes saw the Marines opposite them fan out, she used her hands to instruct those behind her to do the same. They might have come onto *The Faradis* more relaxed than they would for a normal mission, but they had to be on high alert now. A life had been lost; they needed to make sure they didn't lose any more.

The WO had walked off ahead to meet Julius at the large screen in the wall on Reyes' left, so she jogged to catch up to him. Before she realised it, she had Chan beside her.

While Julius pressed the large screen to bring it to life, Reyes looked at her old man. At first he returned a heavy scowl, but his face quickly relaxed. Whether he wanted her on this mission or not, he couldn't change it. Besides, he'd chosen her as his second in command, so he obviously trusted her. He needed to put his personal feelings aside and use her to make this mission a success.

Never one to apologise, he let Reyes back in by speaking to her with less aggression than before. "I need you to make sure you and your team are on high alert. We need to find out what the hell's going on here, and we need to make sure no one else dies."

Before Reyes could reply, Julius turned to face them and said, "Okay, this computer is as locked down as the tablet. The only information I've managed to get out of it is there are three sections, two of them are locked to us—"

"Which we already know," the warrant officer said.

"*But*," Julius replied, "I now think the other sections are closed down because the power's on standby rather than anything more malicious than that."

Chan spoke before the others could. "Then what was the jump to hyperspace about?"

As much as Reyes wanted to pull her in line for the outburst, she didn't. The WO could if he wanted to, but Chan had a point. And she'd saved her life not more than five minutes previously, so she'd earned the right to speak.

At first, Julius shrugged. When no one else spoke, she said, "I don't know. But from looking at the ship now, I'd say this vessel is in hibernation. Maybe the jump was a malfunction."

After he'd looked around at the Marines in the dark and twisted room, the WO turned back to Julius. "How long do you need to get the power back up?"

Several more taps against the screen, Julius shrugged. "Ten minutes, maybe a little bit more. I reckon I'll have control of the ship's comms by then too."

"So even if we can't use my computer to contact the *Crimson Destroyer* …"

"I should be able to do it from here," Julius confirmed. "I'm hopeful I can get a distress signal out at the very least."

The warrant officer pressed the button on the side of his helmet, Reyes flinching as she heard him both in front of her and amplified through her headset. "Julius needs ten minutes. Simpson, come here."

Simpson ran over to them, halting in front of the WO and stamping her foot with a hard slam while saluting him. "Yes, sir?"

"I want you to stay here with Julius. Keep an eye out so she can focus on the computer."

Another stamp on the floor, she saluted him again and moved next to Julius. Her semi-automatic blaster in a two-handed grip, she pressed her back to the wall and faced out across the room.

The warrant officer pressed the button on his headset again. "The rest of us need to search this place. We still have a library, dry food store, briefing room, and sports hall to check out in this main section. While Julius works on getting us off this ship, I want to find out as much as we can about it. Remember, there's no place for speculation. We don't need to be telling each other ghost stories while we deal with searching this vessel. Stay in the same teams. Reyes, you take your seven down the same corridor you just walked down. I'll take mine the other way, and we'll meet you in the library."

Although Chan turned and walked away, before Reyes could follow her, her dad clamped a heavy hand on her shoulder and squeezed it with a hard grip. So tight, she almost twisted away from it. "Lombardo's death wasn't your fault. Those lost on Q328 weren't your fault either." Maybe he knew how much she'd needed to hear that. "I believe in you," he said as he gently shoved her away from him. "Now go and do what you're best at."

Reyes nodded as he turned his back on her. She would have replied were it not for the lump in her throat.

# CHAPTER 20

N ow they were back out in the organically twisted corridor, Reyes took the lead with Chan beside her. It felt strange to be so close to the feisty Marine without them sniping at one another. Although the tension hung so thick between them, the slightest spark could usher the status quo back in.

Despite having a torch on the end of her gun—which Reyes thrust out ahead of her, viewing the corridor from down the barrel of it—it didn't make much difference. The red emergency lighting gave off enough of a glow to negate the torches' effects, but not so much that it afforded them a clear view of where they were heading. They had no way of knowing if anything lurked in the darkness in front of them. But like her father had said: they didn't need to be creating problems that didn't exist.

With so much of her attention in front of her and squinting to see into the gloom in case anything burst from it, Reyes didn't look behind. But she didn't need to. She listened to the pad of the Marines following her as Patel took up the rear again. Of all of them, she trusted him the most with her life.

At the double doors to the library, Reyes stopped to see they looked no different to the other doors they'd encountered so far.

Embedded in the twisted black walls, they were the only constant in what appeared to be a ship created by chance rather than design. When she turned around to face the others, she watched them all flinch away from the bright glare of her torch. "Sorry." She quickly lowered it, pointing the beam at the ground. "I wasn't thinking. We're going to go into the library. I want us to enter it two at a time and spread out if we can. We don't know what we're going to walk into, and after the control room, I want us to be prepared for anything. But like the WO said, don't create problems that don't exist. Chan and I will go in first, and I'll direct you from there. Patel?"

The Marine leaned out so he could see around the others.

"I want you to stay in the corridor and cover our backs."

"Roger that."

The compliance in Patel's reply caught Reyes off guard. Since they'd left Q328, he'd treated her with much more respect. It took some getting used to. To Chan, she said, "You ready for this?"

"Just get on with it, yeah? I'll hold your hand if that'll make it easier for you."

"Screw you, Chan." While glaring at the short Marine, Reyes slammed her hand against the button to open the double doors. They parted like all of the others had so far, the *whoosh* of automation obliging them.

Her gun raised to her shoulder, Reyes walked into the room and looked up, half-expecting another monstrous projection. Instead, she saw only darkness—not even the ceiling. It appeared to stretch impossibly high, higher than it had in any other part of the ship they'd seen so far. After pointing the barrel of her blaster up to better assess it, she got another reminder of just how pathetic their torches were in the dark space.

"This doesn't make sense," Chan said, looking up with Reyes' torch beam. "The ceiling looks to be higher than the ship itself."

If she'd had anything useful to offer in response, Reyes would have. Not only did the space above them seem to go on forever, but between them and the door on the other side—the door her dad and his squad would enter through—stood what looked to be a complex maze of shelves. Tens of them, each one sprang from the floor and ran all the way up into the impossible darkness. They were arranged at different angles, chaotic in their placement. Dark pathways existed between them, but she couldn't see where they led from her current position. The shelves shimmered as both the glow of the Marines' torches and the red emergency lights reflected off the glass fronts covering them.

A finger pressed to the microphone on the side of her helmet, Reyes said, "Sir, are you in position?"

"In the process of it. We're entering the room and spreading out."

"Roger that. We are too." Another click of the microphone button to turn it off, Reyes returned her focus to her team. "Chan and I are going left. Austin and Jacobs, you come in next and go right. Singh and Hunt, stay in the middle. Patel, are you sure you're okay out in the corridor? We don't want to be surprised by something following us in."

"I'm sure," Patel said.

Because the shelves were a few metres away, it gave them a narrow bar of space that stretched the width of the room. Reyes and Chan walked over so they were next to the left wall, Reyes using her torch for guidance. She watched the sweep of her beam animate the shadows in the pathways leading through the maze of shelves. Other than that, the light offered no insight as to where the pathways led.

Reyes pressed her back against the wall and faced the shelves in front of her. Within a few seconds, she stepped forward a pace. The wall felt both too cold and too uncomfortable because of its gnarly twist. A shudder churned through her at the thought of seared flesh.

When Reyes looked back at the entrance to the room, she saw Austin and Jacobs were already making their way to the right wall while Singh and Hunt held their position by the doors.

As Chan stood on high alert beside her, Reyes said, "Uh, Chan?"

The familiar scowl returned to Chan's face when she looked at her.

"Th-thanks for saving me back there."

"One," Chan said while holding up a finger to count it, "I told you I'm professional and can be trusted. I'm not a liar, unlike you."

"*What?*"

"And two, we still lost a Marine, so while I appreciate you recognising I saved your life, someone died."

Lombardo and many others on Q328—too many, but Reyes couldn't dwell on that now. Another look up at the ceiling as if she'd uncover the trickery at work, she still only saw infinite darkness. She pressed the microphone button again. "We're in position, sir. What do you want us to do?"

"Good, now move forward slowly. I don't know why these shelves are laid out in this way, but I reckon we can walk through them and meet in the middle. Let's see what they're hiding. Move one step at a time and keep your wits."

Reyes looked down the line at the others and saw she had their attention from how all their torches faced her way. Were it not for the glow on the ends of their guns, Austin and Jacobs would be completely hidden in the shadows.

Chan stood ready beside her. Reyes looked at the small Marine, nodded at her, and then walked towards the first shelf loaded with books: the entrance to their side of the maze. Not only did the shelves stretch into infinity, but they had the same strange organic twist to them that characterised the rest of the ship. Zero symmetry or straight edges. Instead, the shelves undulated in waves as if they'd once been alive and had been forced to grow and twist with the movement of the dark magic that spawned them.

Despite the apparent chaos of the shelves' creation, as Reyes drew closer to them, she saw every volume on every shelf looked like they belonged there. Almost as if the shelves had grown to fit the books rather than the other way around.

A blink of white light to her right from where Chan's beam bounced off the glass-fronted shelf, Reyes looked at leather-bound books with gold-leaf script on the spines.

"What language is this?" Chan said.

"I've no idea."

"And what kind of species keeps books in this day and age anyway? Surely a data chip is much more convenient?"

While looking around and up at where the ceiling should be, Reyes shrugged. "I can only guess this place is more a museum than a functioning library. Come on, let's keep moving."

When they were past the first set of shelves and deeper into the maze, Reyes pressed the microphone on the side of her helmet. "WO, how are you getting on?"

Silence.

"WO?"

Still nothing.

"Singh? Austin?"

No matter who Reyes tried to connect with, she couldn't get through to them. "Patel?"

"Yes?"

She relaxed ever so slightly. "Can you contact the others? For some reason, they can't hear me. Over."

A few seconds' pause, Patel came back to her. "Yeah, they can hear me. What do you need me to tell them?"

"Contact the WO and tell him my radio's malfunctioning."

"And Chan's?"

The short Marine pressed the button on the side of her helmet. "WO? Singh? Can you read me? Over." She shook her head.

"Hers is screwed too. Tell the WO we'll keep going and meet in the middle. Tell Singh and Austin what's happening."

"Roger, over and out."

For the first time since Reyes had met her, Chan appeared to have nothing to say. "We just need to keep going, right?" Reyes said.

Chan shrugged, so Reyes led the way.

Like the height of the ceiling, the path through the shelves took them deeper than it had any right to. As if confirming Reyes' thoughts, Chan said, "Surely we should be at the halfway point by now. What's going on with this room?"

Before she could answer, Reyes caught sight of a torch's glint ahead. She broke into a jog and heard Chan's steps follow her.

They rounded the next bend and found the warrant officer with Hicks beside him. "What is this place?" Reyes said.

"I've no idea." He scratched his thick stubble while looking around them. "Your guess is as good as mine."

"I think it's an optical illusion," Hicks said. "The shelves are probably painted darker at the top to make the ceiling look taller than it is. The layout of the place probably made us walk in circles without even realising it." His words came quickly and higher in pitch than usual. "Otherwise, this place defies the laws of physics, which we all know it can't do."

It sounded like a question to Reyes, but she didn't answer it. More torches joined them from both sides, and Reyes breathed a relieved sigh to see all four of her team.

When they were all together, the WO said, "Where's Patel?"

"We left him outside in the corridor, watching our backs."

"You did *what?*"

"We left him in the corridor—"

"I heard you. But *why*? Why would you do that?"

While pressing her mic, Reyes said, "Patel, can you hear me?" Nothing.

All of the eyes on her, the tight press of the shelves threw Reyes' high pitch back at her. "We were speaking to him a moment ago." Even as she said it, her stomach dropped. The warrant officer was right; she shouldn't have left a Marine alone.

Reyes spun on her heel and ran from the centre of the maze, the others following her. After just a few metres, she burst out the other side of the shelves. It took a fraction of the effort to get out compared to getting in, but she didn't have time to wonder why. At the exit to the room, she slammed her hand against the button to open it and ran forward. She crashed against the still-closed doors.

Now much closer than she had been when she spoke to him last, Reyes pressed her microphone. "Patel, are you okay out there?"

No reply.

"Patel?"

Still nothing.

A blast exploded from the gloom next to Reyes. She jumped away from the shower of sparks. It left a charred hole where the keypad had been. She turned on Chan and threw her arms in the air. "What the hell was that?"

But Chan didn't respond. Instead, she watched the doors as they opened, and raised her eyebrows.

Without another word, Reyes ran through the doors into the corridor. She used the torch on her gun to look one way and then the other. Because her father and Chan hadn't followed her out, she looked back to see the attention of both of them on her. The rest of their squad gathered around behind them. Not sure how to say it, she shook her head and spoke with a hard exhale. "He's gone."

# CHAPTER 21

R eyes heard the slam of the WO's steps and jumped aside as he marched from the library out into the dark corridor. He wore his usual thick frown, his brow set, and his large frame swayed with his awkward gait. Almost primitive in the way he moved. Not that she'd dare vocalise that assessment of him.

As she watched him look around their immediate area, the need to say something rose in Reyes, but what could she say? Sorry for leaving Patel behind? She thought she was doing the right thing, seeing as the only casualty had come from friendly fire. It was a bit late for that now. Besides, apologies never went down well with the man. Someone who never said sorry himself, he was even worse at accepting apologies than he was at giving them. He seemed to take them as an excuse to stick the boot in harder.

When Chan stepped forward as if she might say something, Reyes put her arm across her chest to restrain her. As they stared at one another, she gently shook her head, calming the situation before the feisty Marine made things worse.

The warrant officer pressed his finger to his headset and

continued to look up and down the crimson-lit corridor as he barked into it, "Patel, where are you?"

Reyes flinched at her dad's loud voice, his clear frustration bubbling over.

A few seconds passed where Reyes could only hear the WO's heavy breaths. The rest of the Marines were silent while they waited for his plan. But how could he make a plan to find Patel if he didn't answer them?

The warrant officer then said, "Julius?"

Although Reyes heard him in her ear again, Julius didn't reply either.

"Shit," he said. "We need to go back to the control room, now. If Julius has gone too, we're screwed."

He set off in the direction of the control room, and Reyes followed on his heels. Chan behind her, she glanced back to see the rest of the Marines file out after them, blasters pressed into shoulders as they remained on high alert.

Just a few short metres to the control room, the WO slapped his hand against the button to open the doors. The sound sent a thunderclap both ways down the dark tunnel, but the doors didn't move. "What the …? What's going on with this ship?" When he turned to Reyes, she might have taken his tone as an accusation had she not known him better. "You walked into and out of these doors earlier, right?"

"We did. They opened fine both times."

Fists like rocks, the WO used his right to bang three hard raps against the doors. He then pressed his microphone again. "Julius?"

Still no reply.

Like she'd done in the library, Chan raised her weapon to shoot the control panel, but Reyes pushed the tip of her gun down and spoke in a whisper. "You might get away with doing that when I'm trying to open the door, but he'll tear your head off if you shoot that thing anywhere near him."

"It worked a minute ago."

"Which he saw. If he wants to shoot it, that's what he'll do."

Despite her words, Reyes had to fight against Chan trying to lift her gun again. "Listen to me. You always call me a daddy's girl, so at least trust me when it comes to making a judgement call about him. You shoot your blaster in his direction and he'll tear your head off, regardless of whether it opens the door or not."

Maybe the warrant officer heard her conversation with Chan, maybe not. Either way, he ignored them both as he raised his hand to knock again. Before he drove his fist against the doors again, the *whoosh* of the mechanism sounded out and the doors parted, revealing Julius on the other side. She looked first at the WO and then poked her head out, her eyes running down the length of the line of Marines all staring back at her.

# CHAPTER 22

When no one spoke, Reyes watched Julius return her attention to the WO directly in front of her. "I feel like you're all waiting for an answer to a question I'm yet to be asked."

"Have you seen Patel?"

"No."

"Did you hear me calling you on the radio?"

"No."

"Did you lock this door and the door to the library?"

"No!"

"Did you hear me knocking?"

"Yes. That's why I opened the door. What's going on?"

The warrant officer used his thick fingers to count their problems out to Julius. "Patel's gone missing, our radios can't reach him or you, and the doors on this damn ship open one minute and then not the next. It's like the thing's got a mind of its own." He flicked a look over his shoulder at those behind him. "And— before anyone suggests it—*no,* I don't think it's haunted, or we've been through the Corinthian's Diamond, or whatever other crap you might want to suggest. I'm just struggling to make sense of all the weird shit."

Although Reyes felt Chan shift her weight next to her as if she'd become uncomfortable where she stood, she didn't take the opportunity to have a cheap dig at her about the Corinthian's Diamond. As much as she wanted to, it wasn't the right time. Instead, she watched Julius and could feel the Marines around her doing the same.

Julius frowned while opening and closing her mouth several times. She scratched her head and winced as if it hurt her brain to try to come up with an answer for the WO.

"Well, at least tell me you've managed to get the system up and running?" he said.

After letting go of a heavy sigh, Julius turned her back on them all, heading towards the computer she'd been working on. Reyes followed directly after Julius and the WO, Chan at her side. The small Marine walked so close to her, she nearly asked her for some space. But if she started an argument at that moment, her father would tear her a new one.

Reyes probably didn't need to say it, but better to be obvious than assume they were all of the same mindset. "Make sure you all come into the room. No one stays behind anymore."

"Actually," Hicks said, "I was planning on camping out in the corridor on my own. Just for shits and giggles, you know?"

The warrant officer spun around to face him. An old dog ready to bite, it snapped a stripe of tension up Reyes' back as she waited for him to cut loose on the facetious Marine.

Thankfully, Julius spoke before he could let rip. "It's going to take a little bit longer to hack this computer than I first thought." Despite addressing the WO, she kept her back to him as she continued across the wide room. Simpson remained on guard next to the brightly lit screen. She looked like she hadn't moved since they'd left her there. Her spine rigid from standing at attention, she looked ready to die for Julius should she need to.

"How much longer?" the WO asked.

"Another ten minutes, maybe more. It's tech I've never seen before. I'm making headway, but I'm having to work it out as I go."

The screen Julius had been working at had lines of blue writing across it. Reyes hadn't ever seen it before, so she looked around the shadowy room instead. The red bulbs did little to light the large space. The shadows in the corners seemed thicker than they had the last time they were in there, almost as if they were closing in on them.

Frustration rode on the back of the warrant officer's low growl. "Can you tell me what's going on with our headsets at least?"

Julius stopped and removed her helmet, examined it for a second, and then looked at the WO's. "The channel on yours is different to mine. It's changed for some reason."

"Some reason?"

"My guess is we've passed through a magnetic field that's messed with it in some way."

"Can a magnetic field make Marines disappear?" Hicks said.

They all knew Hicks well enough to understand he didn't know how to keep a lid on it, especially when he felt nervous. If he felt something, everyone knew about it. Although the WO threw him a sideways glance, he continued his conversation with Julius. "And you can fix it?"

"Easily. If everyone pulls together, I'll do it in one hit rather than separately."

When he turned to the Marines, he saw he didn't need to relay the information. As they clustered together, Julius pulled the warrant officer's tablet from her back pocket.

"I thought that thing was useless?" he said.

"It is if we want to contact any satellites. But I can use it to control anything local, like these headsets."

While Julius fixed their radios, Reyes looked past her at the shadows in the room beyond. It looked like it had grown darker than when they were last in there. A cold chill turned through her. She returned her attention to Julius, who typed against the screen of the tablet before delivering a definitive tap. She then pressed her finger against the microphone button on the side of her helmet and said, "Can everyone hear me now?"

"Loud and clear," Reyes said, looking around to see all the other Marines nodding along with her.

Some of the tension Reyes had seen in her dad's thick frame left him. "Well, that's that sorted at least. A problem fixed with rationale rather than witchcraft. Now we just need to find out where—"

The voice cut him off. Childlike in its soft daydream tone, Reyes recognised it as Patel, but not like she'd heard him before. It sounded haunted and delirious, like he was singing in his sleep.

"Ring-a-ring o' roses, a pocket full of posies, a-tishoo! A-tishoo! We all fall down."

While he sang, many of the Marines—including the WO—stood slack jawed and threw glances at those around them. Things lurked in the shadows of this ship. They all knew it, but because they didn't have anything concrete, they had no proof, so they couldn't vocalise it. The warrant officer didn't want to hear about their fears. Not that it stopped Hicks. "What the hell was that?"

Patel's voice came through to them again as he continued singing. "Ring-a-ring o' roses, a pocket full of posies, hush, hush, hush, hush, we've all fallen down. We've all fallen down. We've all fallen down. We've all fallen down."

Then silence. Even Hicks had nothing this time.

"Patel?" the WO shouted into his microphone, his finger

pressed so hard against the side of his helmet, the tip of it had turned white. "Patel, where are you? What's going on?"

His scowl suggested he either wanted someone to blame, or someone to give him an answer. He glared at Hicks but addressed them all. "What was that?"

Reyes looked at the tight-lipped Marines around her. Why would anyone reply to her father? In his current frame of mind, they'd be walking a tightrope if they even tried to offer him an explanation.

"Does anyone know what Patel was just singing?"

Closed mouths and blank stares, Reyes joined many of the others in looking at the floor.

It took for Julius to turn away from the ship's computer to break the silence. "It's a nursery rhyme from Earth."

"What?"

"I studied human history at college. From what I can remember, the song has something to do with a plague in an ancient city called London. The ring of roses was the rash. They thought posies warded off the disease, so they stuffed their pockets with them."

The warrant officer drew a breath to respond, but Julius cut him off. "It was a long time ago. The sneezing was a symptom of the plague. For those who got it, which was most people in the city at the time … well, they all fell …" She left it hanging.

Although Patel's voice had gone, the echo of *we've all fallen down, we've all fallen down, we've all fallen down* ran through Reyes' mind as if he hadn't.

Without a word, Chan broke away from the group and walked off towards a corner of the room. Her movements were slightly stilted as if she were driven by a will other than her own.

Before Reyes could call after her, the WO shouted, "*Chan!*" The loud syllable snapped through the room. Reyes and many of those around her jumped at the sound of it. But Chan continued to walk over to the corner as if she hadn't heard him.

When she got there, she shone her torch on the floor. She turned back around to face the others, but Reyes already knew what she'd say, dread plummeting through her at the realisation of it. In spite of the swelling and her face being bathed in the red glow of emergency lighting, the colour had left Chan's skin. She looked like she couldn't get her words out. Were Reyes not as knocked over by what she saw too, she might have said it for her.

Finally, Chan cleared her throat and spoke with a warble in her voice. "Lombardo's body is gone."

# CHAPTER 23

E ven Reyes—who'd known him all her life—hadn't seen the
WO lose his head often. Despite his gruff exterior and curt
delivery, he usually either found the solution to a problem, or
found the person with the solution. Q328 had been an anomaly.
Had she not been his daughter, he would have trusted her sooner
than he had. But as she watched him now—his face red and a
large vein raised along his neck—she felt the flutter of panic
disrupting her breaths. None of the rookies around him had an
answer, and he looked like he sure as hell didn't have one himself.
After running his hand over the top of his head, pulling his thick
hair back, he let his frame sag with a slump and stared at the floor.
When he looked back up again, he had the eyes of a predator and
his voice shook. "Now I'm sure I'm being simple, but how can a
body just vanish? What were you two doing?"

A certain confidence that came with her size, Julius pulled her
shoulders back and straightened her spine. "*I* was working on the
computer."

He spun on Simpson. "So *you're* the one to blame?"

Simpson turned to meet his glare, a deep set to her features.
"Nothing came or went while you were gone."

The warrant officer's mouth made a clopping sound as it fell open. He looked from Simpson to Chan in the corner of the room. When he looked back at Simpson, he tilted his head to one side. "So, what? Lombardo just got up and walked out of here?"

"*No!*"

"Well, *something's* happened. When we left, you had a corpse in the corner. Now you don't. It's quite hard to misplace a body— especially an inanimate one."

Not that Simpson would have been able to hear her thoughts, but Reyes silently willed her to keep her mouth shut. Let him vent rather than dig a deeper hole for herself. Thankfully, Simpson read the situation and didn't reply. Instead, she raised her chin and stared straight ahead like she had when they'd first come into the room. She'd remain at Julius' side and continue to watch out for her until ordered to do otherwise.

"And why was the door locked?" he demanded, directing his question at Julius this time.

The tall Marine remained stoic. For a few more seconds, the two locked stares with one another before Julius finally said, "It's only a guess, but I reckon me trying to hack into their controls is having some kind of effect on the ship. Probably just a couple of small malfunctions triggering doors to lock."

"And interfering with our comms?"

"Maybe."

Although he didn't look around, he slightly relaxed his stance as if he'd suddenly become aware of the attention on him. Maybe he simply realised he'd gain little from shouting at people. "It doesn't explain Lombardo though, does it?"

"Look, WO, I really don't know what's happening. What I do know is the sooner I get control of the ship's computer, the more control I'll have over the ship itself. I don't mean to speak out of turn, but Lombardo was dead. We're still alive. All of us are getting the jitters and, I think, rather than me trying to speculate on what's happened to her corpse, I'd be best utilised trying to get a message to the *Crimson Destroyer* so we can all get the hell out of here."

Returning to the man she knew so well, Reyes watched her dad take a few seconds to think. He then nodded. "You're right. Thank you."

Radio static buzzed through Reyes' ear, making her heart kick. When she looked at the other Marines, she saw her own shock staring back at her in many pairs of wide eyes. Patel sang at them again. "Ring-a-ring o'roses, a pocket full—" The lethargy left his voice and he shouted, "I'm *singing!* I'm doing what you told me. What more do you—arghhhhhhhh—" The communication cut off mid-scream.

Reyes looked at Julius to see what she'd done, but she saw the same pallid wash to her face as she saw on the others'. She'd clearly had nothing to do with cutting the comms.

A haunted look in his eyes, the WO said, "Julius is right about Lombardo: she's already dead. It's not that I don't care, but rescuing a corpse is less important than getting to Patel. Julius, give me a time. How long do you need?"

"Another ten minutes."

"Another ten?"

Julius shrugged.

"Right." While holding his wrist up, the warrant officer pressed his watch, the screen lighting up. "All of you set ten-minute timers. We're going to search this ship for Patel. Whatever happens, I want everyone back here in ten—with Patel or not. I don't trust our comms will remain online, so make sure you're all keeping an eye on your watches. No excuses for being late. Reyes?"

Reyes set her watch—an awareness of the others doing the same around her—before she flicked her head up to look at him. "Sir?"

"Take your team down the same corridor you were in. We're going to search the rooms in this main section."

"But that will take longer than ten minutes."

"Not if we split up. Make sure no one's on their own, but if we enter each room from either side in teams of two or more, we should be able to check out all of the rooms and be back in time."

While trying to hide her slight tremble, her gut tightening, Reyes nodded at her dad. They had to find Patel—whatever it took—and with ten minutes to kill, it seemed like a productive use of their time. Despite her reservations, staying in the control room while Julius hacked the ship's computer wouldn't help anyone.

To the rest of the Marines, he said, "Unless anyone else has something they want to add, we need to move out. Let's find our brother, get back here, contact the *Crimson Destroyer*, and then get the hell off this damned ship."

He made it sound so simple.

# CHAPTER 24

B ack in the corridor they'd lost Patel in, Reyes called back to the four Marines behind her, Chan by her side again. "Stay in pairs and keep an eye on your partner. Remember what the WO said: we come back in ten minutes, and we *all* return—no matter what. We don't need heroes today."

"That's a shame," Chan said as she brought her torch up and shone it in Reyes' face, "especially when we have a bona fide one leading us. What are we going to do with all that hero power?"

"And there's me thinking you'd grown up. That you'd realised our safety was more important than your petty grudges."

Although Chan smiled, the red emergency lighting and the swelling on her face did their best to dilute the effect. She looked part gargoyle. "Looks like I've found a way to do both."

A shake of her head, Reyes pointed her gun—and torch by extension—out in front of her and set off down the gloomy and red-lit corridor. The wet shine of the metal glinted as if the ship perspired. The last time she'd walked this way, she'd spent most of her effort trying to see all the way to the end. It had been a fruitless task, so this time she looked at her immediate surroundings, doing her best to ignore Chan's smug face in her peripheral vision.

"So when will you admit you're a fake, Reyes?"

"What's with you? When are you going to let this nonsense drop? I'm not bragging about Q328. You heard what happened, and a lot of good Marines died. Who'd come back from that feeling like a hero?"

"It's not Q328 I'm talking about."

Reyes stopped and shone her torch—and gun by extension—in Chan's face. "So enlighten me."

All the mirth had abandoned Chan, her eyes narrowing as her voice dropped. "I think you know."

"Look, whatever petty argument you have in mind, drop it, yeah? This isn't about you right now. I'm trying to find any clue as to where Patel has gone. My main focus is finding him."

"Don't question my professionalism."

"You make it hard not to."

This time, Chan chose to keep quiet. In the silence, the memory of Patel's voice haunted Reyes' every step. His eerie and childlike singing sounded nothing like the man she knew. What was happening to him?

They reached the doors to the library without incident. When Reyes hit the button for them, they opened immediately. Were she next to anyone but Chan, she might have made a comment about it. Instead, she pressed the mic on the side of her helmet. "WO, are you there?"

"I'm here, Reyes. What's up?"

The door still opened wide in front of her, the room seemed darker than before. The same tall shelves dominated the space, creating what looked like an organic maze of twisted metal, but the shadows seemed heavier somehow, the emergency lighting duller. Probably just her imagination. "We're at the library. Where are you?"

"The library."

While looking at the two Marines directly behind her, she said, "I'm going to send Austin and Hunt in."

"Okay." Reyes then listened to him take over the main channel. "Hicks, Platt, I need you two to go in here. Austin and Hunt are coming in from the other side. I need you to meet them in the middle. Search the place together and make sure Patel isn't in there. If we lose contact, I want you back in the control room in ten minutes. No excuses. And make sure all four of you return."

Someone snorted a cynical laugh.

"Do you have a problem, Hicks?" the warrant officer said.

"I'd say we all have a problem, sir."

"So stop making it worse."

"Yes, sir."

While Hicks and the WO were talking to one another, Reyes watched Austin pull in a deep breath. A normally upbeat person with a quick wit and good sense of humour, she saw none of that in him at that moment. As he walked past her into the library, she patted him on the back. Hunt followed behind him. "We'll be off this ship in no time," she called into the room after them. Even her echo struggled to penetrate the shadows, the sound of her voice dying in the darkness. Neither Marine replied. Not that she could blame them. They'd all been in the library. It could well be the worst room on the ship, and she'd chosen not to go in herself. But better the devil they knew; at least they'd seen the inside of it. The stars only knew what waited for them in the other rooms.

# CHAPTER 25

After the doors to the library had closed, Reyes shut her eyes for a second as if the action would somehow offer her a moment of respite. When she opened them again, she found Chan standing directly in front of her. While maintaining eye contact, Reyes pressed the mic on the side of her helmet. "Are you ready to move on, sir?"

"We're already moving. We have less than nine minutes left."

Farther into the ship than they'd been before, Reyes pushed on. The corridor looked no different. The same hellish twist that resembled burned reptilian flesh. The same shimmer from the glossy surface. The same turn and roll to her steps. It felt like the deeper they ventured down the corridor, the farther it stretched. Almost as if the ship wanted to prevent them from reaching the end of it.

Chan still at her side, Reyes didn't even want to look at her when they arrived at the dry food stores. She pressed the button, and the doors opened as easily as they had for the library. Although Reyes shone her torch inside, it did little because the same crimson-tinged darkness occupied the room. She could see just about far enough to catch a glimpse of the shelving. The space appeared to be much more conventional than the library. It looked more like a warehouse than a Gothic storage space for arcane literature. "I'm going to go to the end with Chan," Reyes said while staring into the dark, her finger pressed against the microphone button on the side of her helmet.

"Okay," the warrant officer's gruff voice rumbled in her ear. "I'm going to go into this one, then. I'll take Holmes and Niamura in with me. We'll do this room and the briefing room because they're smaller."

"I'm going to send Singh and Jacobs in."

"Have they set their timers?"

When Reyes looked back at the two soldiers, they both nodded. "Yep. See you back in the control room. Take care."

"You too, you'll have Crouch and Grady with you at the end."

A sudden swell of panic caught in Reyes' throat, clamping it tight. She didn't need the responsibility for the Marines on the other side. After coughing, she found her breath again and said, "Roger that. Take care."

Muscles of lead, Reyes pushed on down the corridor. The bounce in Chan's step beside her suggested she didn't feel the same burden. And why should she? She hadn't been given any responsibility.

Reyes and Chan said nothing to one another as they walked past the briefing room. The doors to the sports hall came into sight a few steps later. But before they got to them, the end of the corridor appeared from the shadows, stopping Reyes dead. It might have been irrational, but she hadn't believed it would happen. She let her tense frame relax a little. Of course the corridor had an end. It was exactly why her dad had urged them to only deal with evidence. At no point did she have any proof that the corridor went on forever. If she continued to let panic dictate her thoughts though, she'd get someone killed.

Instead of focusing on the sports hall's entrance on her left,

Reyes looked at the door to her right. It had a number three above it. What did they have in there that Julius' schematics wouldn't show them? Patel? Lombardo's body?

Reyes pressed her mic again. "Crouch?" She chose to speak to him because she knew him better than Grady.

"Reyes?"

"Yep. Can you see a door leading to another section? It'll have a number two above it."

"I can."

Reyes walked over to the number three door, her hand shaking as she pressed the button to open it. It didn't budge. When Chan raised her gun and pointed it at the card reader, Reyes pushed the end of it down like she'd done earlier. Ignoring the daggers Chan stared at her, she then spoke to Crouch again. "Can you open yours?"

After a second, he said, "No."

"No, we can't either." She looked at Chan when she said, "And we don't have time to get distracted by them. Let's leave them for now and get into the sports hall." She checked her watch. "We have six minutes. We can tell the others about these doors when we get back."

"Okay, Reyes, on your mark."

"Three …" Reyes said, checking Chan to make sure she looked ready. She continued to scowl at her.

"Two …"

Chan stepped forward, her hand hovering over the button to open the door.

"One."

When Chan pressed the button, the doors opened with a *whoosh*.

Reyes led the way into the sports hall first, and Chan followed on her heels. "Are you in, Crouch?"

But Crouch didn't respond.

"Crouch?"

Nothing.

A few more steps into the sports hall, Reyes pressed the button on her mic several times as if repeated pressure would somehow inspire it to work better. "Crouch! Answer me. Are you in?" The only thing that replied to her was the echo of her own tense voice.

The whoosh of the door closing sounded opposite them, but when Reyes looked across the hall, she saw nothing, the darkness depriving her of a clear view of the other side. "Crouch?" From what she could see, it looked exactly like a sports hall, an open space much like the arena they played murderball in. Except in here, there were different kinds of goals and markings on the floor, which was the first level surface she'd walked on since boarding the ship. Whatever species the crew of *The Faradis* were, they obviously needed a flat surface to run on. Bathed in the warm red of emergency lighting, it defied logic that she couldn't see to the other side. But like everywhere else on the ship, the shadows didn't seem to adhere to the physics she knew.

When Reyes walked forward, Chan moved with her. They both had their blasters raised and pressed into their shoulders, their torches ineffective as they tried to use them to scan the space in front. They headed straight for the doors on the other side of the room. Or at least where they expected them to be.

As they drew closer and the room's exit became visible, Reyes said, "Where the hell are Crouch and Grady?"

After she'd spun a full circle, Chan shrugged. "They've vanished."

Reyes walked over to one of the dark corners, and Chan followed her. She then walked over to the other one. Nothing.

The alarm on Reyes' watch went off, the high-pitched pip of it calling through the quiet. "That feels like much less than ten minutes." Reyes then pressed her mic again. "WO, we need a few more minutes before we leave the sports hall. Crouch and Grady have gone. We don't yet know where. If anyone has finished searching their section, we could do with a few more bodies down here."

The same silence she'd heard when she'd tried to speak to Crouch and Grady.

"WO?"

Nothing.

An obvious thing to state, but Reyes looked at Chan and stated it anyway. "The radios are down again."

Chan retied her tight ponytail as she continued to take in the room. "The WO's going to lose his shit if we don't go back right now."

"But what about Crouch and Grady?"

"He said no exceptions. And they're clearly not here."

The memories of Q328 … the rock creatures that lived there … the sound of Patel's voice … It all swirled through Reyes' head. "Then where are they? People don't just vanish into thin air."

The alarm on Chan's watch went off, and Reyes stared down at it as it glowed on her wrist. "I thought you set yours at the same time I did?"

"I thought I did too."

Silence for a moment, Reyes said, "I'll wait here in case Crouch and Grady appear. You go and get back up."

"You think I'll leave you down here on your own?"

"Why not?"

"Your dad would kick my arse. I'd gladly leave you to face whatever might come your way, but I don't want to be on the receiving end of his wrath."

"But what are we going to do about Crouch and Grady?"

"What can we do?" Before Reyes could reply, Chan said, "Maybe they've gone back. Maybe they looked at their watches before entering the room and realised how little time they had. The warrant officer was quite explicit about not exceeding the ten minutes he gave us. Maybe they tried to tell you but couldn't because the comms were down."

"You think they would have gone back without telling us?"

"Have you met your dad? Anyone who's late will get it in the neck from him. I think keeping him happy will be their number one priority."

They were by the doors Crouch and Grady should have walked through. Chan pressed the button and they slid open. "Let's go back this way. If they've gone back for any reason, or if they're stuck in this corridor, we can help them."

"But what if something else has happened?" Reyes said.

"There's only one way to find out. It's the only call, Reyes. You can't be a hero here. Come on."

For a moment, Reyes remained rooted to the spot as she watched Chan walk out through the doors.

"Come *on*," Chan said.

"Damn it." Reyes shook her head and walked after the diminutive Chan.

# CHAPTER 26

L ate for their rendezvous, Reyes and Chan jogged up the gloomy corridor to get back to the control room. As she ran, Reyes' feet twisted and turned, the traumatised floor offering no level footing. Maybe they should have been more cautious, but with the WO's wrath waiting for them, the sooner they got back, the better. In balance, the small risk that she could get a broken ankle felt like a worthwhile gamble.

The doors to the control room opened when Reyes hit the button. Even though it had only happened to them twice, she'd already learned to distrust that she'd be granted access to any room on *The Faradis*. Out of breath, she stepped into the space to see many of the Marines had made it back.

The warrant officer stood close to Julius and Simpson by the ship's computer. Simpson stood as rigid as ever, a sentry to protect Julius should she need it. When the WO looked over at Reyes, his usual scowl hooded his eyes. Words raced to the tip of her tongue, a garbled mess about to explode from her mouth. But she didn't know what he intended to ask her. She pulled the words in and took a moment to centre herself. Let him speak first.

"Why have you just come in through *that* door?"

Not the first question she'd expected. She quickly scanned the Marines in the room. Not only were Crouch and Grady missing, but she couldn't see Austin and Hunt either.

"Reyes?"

The snap of his bark pulled her focus back to him.

"Why did you just come in from that side?"

After she'd looked at the Marines in the room to be sure she hadn't missed them, she said, "Where are Crouch and Grady?"

Silence swept through the place before the WO broke it, his deep voice cautious like the low growl of a large dog. "They were in the sports hall with you two."

"But they never entered the room."

"*What?*"

"We were talking to them on the radio when they were in the opposite corridor, but when we entered the sports hall, we lost contact with them and they were nowhere to be seen. The radios died, so we couldn't talk to them."

"Why didn't you look for them?"

The question wound tension through Reyes' back. It took all she had to keep her tone level. Respectful. "We *did*. You think we'd just give up on them?" Before he could answer, she went on to say, "It was an open room. If they were in there, we would have seen them. Then our ten-minute timers went off and we had to get back here." She pointed at the door they'd just come in through. "We came down the other corridor, hoping we'd find them on the way back."

Despite everything she'd told him, the warrant officer said, "Your timers went off? What are you talking about?" After looking at his own watch, he fixed her again with his cold stare. "You still have over two minutes left."

Reyes looked at her watch and noticed Chan do the same. "*Both* of our timers went off, which is why we came back."

This time Julius spoke, pulling herself away from the computer. "You've been gone seven minutes at the most, Reyes."

"Then why did my watch go off?"

"You must have set it wrong."

"And Chan's?"

An apologetic wince, Julius didn't offer an explanation. They must have set their watches wrong. Both of them. And Reyes couldn't argue with her about it. When they were in such a confined space, time could be relied upon as a universal metric. Only when they put galaxies between them did the unreliability of it rear its relative head.

The silence lasted for a few more seconds before Julius turned back to the computer.

The WO took over the conversation again. "Did you lose your nerve? Is that why you didn't wait?"

Chan stepped forward, knocking shoulders with Reyes as she passed her. "With all due respect, *sir*, Reyes wanted to stay. She said she'd wait behind and that I should come and get help. I wouldn't let her do that. I didn't want to leave her on her own. Not in light of what's been happening on this cursed ship."

Reyes flinched as she watched him fill his chest with a deep inhale. But before he could let loose, the watch on his wrist lit up and his alarm sounded.

It took Julius away from the screen again. She looked down at it. "That's going off early too. According to this computer, you still have ninety seconds before the ten minutes are up."

Another scan of the room showed Reyes that Austin and Hunt were still missing. She saw Platt, who'd gone into the library from the other side. "Where are Austin and Hunt?"

"We met in the centre of the library, and both pairs left along different routes. We didn't have the time to search every path through the maze if we remained as a group of four."

"And how long have you been back here for?"

"Three or four minutes."

"So they should be back by now?"

Platt dropped his gaze to the floor. "I don't want to freak anyone out."

"I think we're already freaked out, Platt. Didn't you hear Patel earlier?"

No reply. And what could he say to her? While looking from one door to the other as if her attention would somehow make the missing Marines appear, Reyes chewed on her bottom lip. Before she could ponder it any further, the crimson glow of the room gave way to a brilliant white glare. It shone so brightly she stumbled back a few steps and covered her eyes against its burning assault.

# CHAPTER 27

I t took at least a minute of Reyes blinking repeatedly and rubbing her eyes before her sight returned. Many of the others looked like they hadn't gotten there yet, staring around them like blind pups searching for a teat. In that moment, she took in the intricacies of the room and her blood ran cold. Where she'd seen an approximation of the place in the deep red glow of the emergency lighting, she now got to take it in with an entirely new perspective. The comparison of the metal to melted flesh rang truer than ever: melted flesh that had knotted back together in a feeble attempt to regain some of its original form, failing miserably and offering an onyx sight of torment and nightmares.

Before anyone could ask what had happened, Julius indirectly gave them the answer, "*Crimson Destroyer*, this is Julius on *The Faradis*. Do you read me?"

The reply came back almost instantly. Farrell, the *Crimson Destroyer*'s second in command, said, "Julius, thank the stars. We've been trying to get hold of you. Are you okay?"

"Yes." Then Julius looked at the Marines and sighed. "Ish. Look, we need to get off here ASAP. Can you track us and come now?"

A few seconds of silence before Farrell replied. "How the hell did you get that far away?"

"The ship jumped into hyperspace. We had no control where it went. Can you come to us?"

"Yes, but we need some time. We're going to have to do three jumps at least."

"How long?"

"We can get to you in an hour."

Another moment of silence as Julius looked at the warrant officer. He shrugged. What else could he do?

"Please get here as quickly as you can," Julius said.

"Will do. Oh, and we can't stay there for long."

"What do you mean?"

"You're in the middle of an unstable part of space. There are meteor showers and black holes everywhere. It's a huge risk coming in at all. I reckon we've got three minutes at the most before we put the *Crimson Destroyer* in too much jeopardy. I'm going to have to programme for us to jump in and out again three minutes later. We can't attach ourselves to *The Faradis* either because we don't want it clinging onto us or dragging us into a black hole. You have to get to the escape pods and come to us."

"And what if we can't do that?" Julius said.

"Then we can't get you out of there. We have no flexibility on it. It's not somewhere I'd dream of taking a ship into normally. Sorry."

Julius looked at the WO while she replied, "You can only do what you can do. We'll make sure we're ready."

Reyes saw the warrant officer nod at her comment.

"Okay. Hang on in there. Over and out."

The mood in the room plummeted the second the *Crimson Destroyer* cut the conversation. Reyes' own body slumped where she stood.

The loud snap of the WO clapping his hands once pulled the

room's attention onto him. He walked into the middle of the space, one of his steps hitting the twisted black metal floor harder than the other on account of his limp. "We need to be positive here. We're going to get rescued. We have an hour to find the escape pods, the five missing Marines, and Lombardo's body."

The high pitch of Hicks' voice took flight through the room. His facetious tones had given way to straight-up panic. "And what if we can't get to the escape pods and we miss the three-minute window?"

"We won't."

Although Hicks looked like he wanted to say more, the doors on Reyes' left made a whopping sound as they opened. Every Marine in the room turned to face them, many of them drawing their weapons.

When Austin entered with Hunt behind him, he smiled. "Wow, what a welcoming party. You lot must have been super quick to get back so soon. We thought we'd be the first to return."

None of the Marines spoke, so Austin held his wrist up. The light on his watch then came on with the sound of his alarm. "We beat the ten minutes."

Reyes and the warrant officer looked at one another before he turned to Julius. "What the hell's going on?"

# CHAPTER 28

Austin turned his alarm off while the WO continued to look at Julius. "How long was that one?"

Although Julius didn't turn around from the computer, Reyes saw her lift her eyes to check the top of the screen. "About eleven minutes."

"Why are they all so different?" Every time he asked a question, his voice got louder, and Reyes watched his face redden. The bright glare of the lights above left no room for misinterpretation.

Reyes watched Julius' back tense in the face of the warrant officer's inquisition. She remained focused on the screen. "Uh," she said, "I'm not sure. There are a lot of things happening on this ship that I have no explanation for. This is all new to me too."

"Make a guess."

Maybe Reyes should step in. Julius clearly didn't have an explanation for all the strange events, and he must have seen that. But, as always, when it came to speaking to her old man, her tongue felt too fat for her mouth and the words lodged in her throat.

"If … if I had to guess, I would say it's the same thing that's messing with our comms."

"Magnetic fields?"

For the first time since the WO had pursued this line of questioning, Julius turned away from the screen to look at him. Her brows rose in the middle and she shrugged. "It's the best I have."

An already thick jaw tightened as he finally pulled his attention from Julius and turned a slow circle, taking in the room. When his eyes fell on Reyes, he stopped. Maybe he knew she had something to say; he didn't look like he wanted to hear it. He maintained eye contact with her and addressed all of them. "I suppose we need to make use of this time. At least we now only have three Marines and a corpse to find. That's progress, right?"

After a second or two, he looked back at Julius. "What if the ship jumps into hyperspace again? Can you do anything to stop that?"

"I can, but—"

"I don't want to hear a 'but'; if there's any chance this damn ship could take us to the arse end of the galaxy again, I want to prevent it. *Whatever* it takes. We need to make sure we're here when the *Crimson Destroyer* turns up."

The turmoil on Julius' face suggested she had more to say, so Reyes stepped forward to advocate for her. She'd held her tongue with her dad too many times. She was an adult now and he had to listen to her. Besides, it looked like whatever Julius had to say, they needed to hear it. Before she spoke, Chan stepped towards her.

The small Marine had obviously seen Reyes' intention because she shook her head almost imperceptibly. No one wanted to put their neck on the line with the warrant officer in his current mood—even more reason for her to do it. Playing the daughter card sometimes worked in her favour.

Julius tried one more time. "Just please let me explain wh—"

"*Whatever* it takes," the WO said.

Maybe Julius had sensed she had an advocate in Reyes

because she looked directly at her as if silently pleading for her to step in. Chan's advice in her mind, the need to intervene both rose and died in her. She couldn't do it. A quick glance at the others and it didn't look like anyone else wanted to do it either. The warrant officer had made up his mind. Whatever meant whatever, and if she spoke out, he'd slam her down in front of everyone there.

A heavy sigh sagged through Julius before she burst to life. Moving in one fluid motion, she drew her blaster, aimed it at the screen in front of her, and pulled the trigger.

The loud *pop* made Reyes jump. If the wide-eyed Marines around her were anything to go by, she wasn't the only one.

Where the monitor had glowed with backlit brilliance, it now fizzed, popped, and kicked out sparks that landed on the dark floor and died.

However long passed before the warrant officer spoke, every painful second of silence twisted through Reyes. She should have said something.

"Oh," the WO finally said while scratching his beard. "That's what you wanted to explain to me."

"It's the only way to disable the hyperdrive. Now while this ship has many surprises, from what I can ascertain, it only has one control computer. Breaking that should stop it making another jump until it's fixed."

"*Should?*"

Julius shrugged.

So quiet in the room, Reyes heard the sound of the warrant officer scratching his beard again. He then said, "But the *Crimson Destroyer* definitely knows where we are?"

"Yep."

"Then it doesn't matter that we can't access the computer again, right?"

Julius shrugged. "Right. Also, it would take me days to properly crack their systems to shut down the hyperdrive, so any more time on the computer would be a waste anyway. There's not much else I can do with—"

Before Julius could finish, several heavy clunks ran through the ship. They started far away from them. Hard to tell, but if Reyes had to guess, she'd say they started in the sports hall. What she could tell for sure was each one drew closer. *Thunk. Thunk. Thunk.*

Many of the Marines raised their blasters and faced one of the two doors. Austin and Hunt did the same while stepping away from the door they'd just walked through, moving closer to the others.

The next *thunk* turned the control room red, the bright lights giving way to the crimson glow of a ship on emergency power.

Two more loud *thunks* moved farther up the ship. Then silence reigned again.

"You could have turned the lights back on though, right?" the WO said.

Julius didn't reply. Reyes should have intervened when she had the chance.

Before anyone could say anything else, there was a scream in the corridor outside.

# CHAPTER 29

The scream came from the corridor Reyes and Chan had just walked down. Although the Marines had their weapons raised, none of them moved towards the door. Instead, they all looked at the WO. Without a word, he pressed the butt of his blaster into his shoulder and took slow steps towards the sound.

Many of the Marines remained rooted to the spot. While walking with her dad, Reyes wanted to yell at them. One of their own was in trouble and they were too scared to move! She'd seen too many die already; she had to remember that most of them hadn't.

Another scream lifted gooseflesh all over Reyes' body. Now closer to the doors—the other Marines finally closing in around them—she heard a voice. It was Crouch. He shouted, the screech of his voice making her swallow with empathy for how it must have hurt his throat. "Why me? What have I done to deserve this?"

The WO slammed a heavy whack against the button to open the doors, but they didn't budge. He hit it so hard the second time, the slapping sound clapped through the dark room. He yelled out and drove a hard fist against the resolute barrier. It felt like his blow against the doors shook the entire ship, but they didn't budge.

Maybe Crouch had an awareness of them coming, because Reyes heard him call out, "Please, just fucking end it. Don't leave me like this."

Before the warrant officer could hit the button again, Reyes shot the control panel in the wall. Sparks exploded away from it as it shattered, but the doors didn't budge.

He spun on her, his furrowed brow a mess of hard lines. The rest of the room looked at her too.

Crouch's scream came again, pulling everyone's attention back to the locked doors. "Help me!"

Reyes spun around and set off in the opposite direction. She shoved past Austin and Hunt, who loitered at the back of the group. When she hit the button next to the double doors on the other side of the room, they slid open for her.

"What are you doing, Reyes?" the WO yelled after her.

She called back to him as she sprinted from the room into the blood-red corridor beyond. The doors were already closing behind her. "I'm getting to Crouch. He's there because I left him behind. I'm going to get to him before it's too late. We're not going to lose any more of our people."

The doors to the control room were already closed as Reyes ran down the dark and twisted corridor—her feet turning with the roll of the uneven floor—but she heard the footsteps of the others giving chase. She couldn't slow down. It sounded like seconds would make all the difference to Crouch.

The doors to the library opened as easily as the ones from the control room had, and Reyes charged straight in.

Until that moment, Reyes had forgotten just how dark the room was compared to all the others. A few steps in, she halted and looked at the shelves. Like before, they stretched from floor to ceiling and took up most of the space. But they looked different somehow, like they'd been rearranged. As she took them in again, she nodded to herself. They *had* been rearranged. Where there had been multiple entry points to the maze the last time she'd been in the room, she now only saw one. It ran a path straight through the centre of the space.

Still rooted to the spot, her jaw wide, she said, "What the hell is this ship?" Then she heard Crouch scream even louder than before. She took off again, sprinting down the pathway through the centre of the shelves.

Despite the change in layout, the same twisted black metal housed what looked to be the same ancient tomes, and the room had the same tormented architectural aesthetic. When Reyes had gone through the shelves the first time, she wouldn't have been able to retrace her steps, so what did it matter if she had a new route now? The fact remained that she needed to get to Crouch on the other side.

The slap of Reyes' feet beat against the metal floor. When the sound of her steps grew louder, she couldn't tell if they were her own being thrown back at her or if the others had followed her into the room. She'd learned a lot about Chan since they'd boarded *The Faradis*. No doubt she'd be on her heels, and if she ran after her, the others would too.

There might have been a hellish twist to the maze, but the path through it ran in a straight line. Reyes burst from the other side without incident and kept moving at a sprint towards the doors. But when she tried to press the button, she saw the panel had already been shot. "Huh?"

A bang slammed against the other side, and Reyes jumped back from it. Her heart, overworked from the run, beat even harder from the shock. Short and rapid breaths, she tried to ride it out. "Crouch?"

"Reyes?"

"*Chan?* You managed to get into the other corridor! How's Crouch?"

The door muffled Chan's words, but Reyes heard her just fine. She wished she hadn't. "What are you talking about?"

"The door the WO was trying to operate. The one I shot in the control room. You got it open?"

"*No*. We followed you." Several slaps rang out from the other side of the door, where Chan was clearly trying to open it with the button. Then Reyes heard the pulse of laser fire and the fizz of breaking electrical wires. It made no difference.

"But how?" Reyes had run in a straight line through the maze of shelves. She hadn't turned once.

"Are you okay, Reyes? How did you get in? The doors are locked."

"They weren't when I pressed the button a few seconds ago." It suddenly made sense why the panel on her side had already been shot. Chan had shot it to get them out of the room the last time they were in there.

A tremble ran through Reyes. She opened her mouth to speak, but Crouch's call cut her off. As far away as before, getting to him had to be her priority. Maybe she couldn't have done anything on Q328, but she could do something now.

Chan continued to beat against the other side of the door as Reyes took off towards Crouch in another attempt to reach him. Then she looked at the shelves again and stopped. They were laid out like they'd been the first time they were in there. Not the straight line through the middle of a few seconds ago, but multiple entry points. She stepped back until she leaned against the door, the vibration of Chan's thuds running through her back. As much as she wanted to call out for help, she'd gotten herself into this mess. And what could the others do anyway? If they couldn't open the doors, they couldn't open them. No amount of whining would change that.

While resting against the cold metal, Reyes heard Crouch again. His voice came through to her from the other side of the room, navigating the maze as if it were nothing. "Just end it now. *Please.*"

If nothing else, she had to at least try to save him. Reyes sprinted towards the shelves, aiming for the path down the centre of the room, which was now more twisted than before.

It took for the echo of the tight space to make Reyes realise she was crying. Crying for Crouch. Crying for her own fear. Crying for those lost on Q328. The close tunnel threw her gasping grief back at her in erratic and stuttered bursts. She turned left, right, left, right, right, right, left.

When she emerged from the other side of the shelves this time, she looked straight at the panel beside the door. It remained intact. Before she got close enough to press it, she heard Chan's banging as she called after her. The sounds came from the other side of the shelves. She'd definitely made it through this time.

Reyes winced as she pressed the button to open the doors. They parted immediately. She let go of a hard exhale while stumbling forwards into the dark corridor. For the briefest of moments, she convinced herself she'd gotten through the worst of it. Crouch's wild scream reminded her she hadn't even scraped the surface.

Then she saw him.

Crouch lay on his back on the glistening, obsidian floor. Too dark in the corridor for Reyes to see all the gruesome details, but not dark enough to take the impact of his suffering away. His eyes were wide as he looked up at her, his mouth bent out of shape. The glistening shimmer of his own wet blood covered his face, and he held something in both of his hands. Two hands didn't look to be enough to contain it all. The pile slipped and spilled over as he tried to balance his recently liberated innards.

Reyes crouched down in front of him, turning her face away

from the rich kick of excrement snaking up her nostrils—excrement and the copper reek of his spilled blood.

"Reyes," he said between gasps, his entire frame trembling. "Grady ... he's gone."

While stroking his hair away from his forehead, her hand turning damp with his blood, Reyes said, "Where? What's happened to him?"

A hypothermic shake racking his body, Crouch opened and closed his mouth several times, but he couldn't get his words out. Where Reyes had seen stark panic in his wide eyes, a glaze now covered them as if he'd retreated into his skull.

"Crouch," Reyes said, "what's happened? What have you seen?"

A hard spasm bucked through Crouch's frame, his legs snapping straight from the jolt. Then he fell limp.

Still exhausted from her run, Reyes panted as she stared down at the dead Marine. Her legs finally failed her and she fell forwards onto her knees, the cold spread of Crouch's blood soaking into her trousers.

# CHAPTER 30

R eyes didn't know how long they'd been banging for, but the heavy beat of their fists against the other side of the door helped coax her away from her own internal hell. Still kneeling in the obsidian corridor, she lifted her gaze from Crouch's corpse. Her tears blurred the details of her crimson-hued surroundings. Her cheeks were soaked with her grief, her trousers with Crouch's blood. The cold press of it lay against her knees as a damp reminder of another expired Marine.

The banging came again, pulling a gasp from Reyes and helping her refocus on it. She stared at the control room door, the one she'd tried to open from the other side when they'd first heard Crouch scream.

Before Reyes could speak, she heard another impatient knock. This time, her father's voice came through with it. "Reyes? What's going on out there?"

As much as she wanted to call back to him, Reyes couldn't get the words past the lump in her throat. She pressed her hand against the cold metal wall beside her to help her stand. The feel of the undulated surface made her shudder, the image of burned reptilian skin crashing to the front of her currently febrile mind.

On her feet, Reyes stumbled towards the door on wobbly legs. Her hand shook as she reached out to press the button to open it. If it didn't budge, she'd be screwed. While holding her breath, she pressed it. The tension fell from her body to watch it slide open. Not even the fierce scowl of the WO surrounded by Marines could quell her relief. She let go of a heavy sigh. "Am I glad to see you lot."

The warrant officer yelled and charged forward. He lifted Reyes by the front of her shirt before slamming her—back first— into the wall opposite him. The hard impact drove the wind from her, and she fell limp in his grip, gasping as she fought to catch her breath. When he let her go, her knees took the brunt of the impact as she fell to the solid and uneven ground. Fire in her kneecaps, she cried harder than before.

The hot breath of the man pressed against Reyes' face as he leaned down at her. She winced away from the blast of his raised voice. "What the hell was that? *Don't* go off on your own. Not on this ship. You think you're a hero because you saw a weakness in the creatures on our last mission? You're not! You're a damn fool."

Reyes' shoulders bounced as she cried freely for the loss of Crouch. Her attention on the floor, she shook her head. It took her several attempts to reply through her gasps. "I had to get to Crouch. I wanted to save him. Too many have died already." She sniffed against her running nose and stared up into her father's eyes. He looked like he wanted to swing for her, but screw him. "I'd do it again in a heartbeat."

The WO's voice dropped so low Reyes could barely hear him. Each word shook like distant thunder, the promise of a storm coming her way. She knew him well enough to know if he cut loose on her now, he wouldn't stop. "Then you'll be *dead* in a heartbeat." The side of his face widened from clenching his jaw as he chewed back his fury. Then she saw the truth behind his rage. A wet glaze spread across his blue eyes. A shake ran through him and his voice broke. "I told you not to come on this damn mission, didn't I?"

Before Reyes could reply, Julius interrupted them. "Um, sir?"

The warrant officer looked over at her. She'd gone down to where Crouch's body had been just moments ago. "Crouch isn't here," she said.

The words cut through Reyes' grief. She turned so quickly her head spun. His blood still on her hands and lying damp against her knees, she stared at where Crouch had been only seconds before and shook her head. "He was *there*. I spoke to him."

Silence settled over the Marines as they all stared at her.

"I'm not imagining it," Reyes said. She held her hands out to show them. They were still coated with Crouch's blood. "See, I watched him die. His stomach was torn open."

Where Reyes expected the WO to say something, he didn't. Instead, he looked down the corridor at Julius for a few seconds before he walked away.

It took two Marines to help Reyes stand. They grabbed her beneath each arm: Chan on one side, Simpson on the other. When they'd gotten her upright, Simpson patted her back before moving off. But Chan leaned close to Reyes. "What the hell was that about? Why did you run off on your own?"

As Reyes stared at Chan, her head cleared, her focus returning. "This ain't the time to be scoring points, you know. If you've come to stick the boot in … don't."

A few seconds of silence between them, Reyes and Chan eyeballed one another before Chan shook her head and stepped off in the direction of the WO. While watching her walk away, Reyes balled her fists.

Neither the warrant officer nor Chan went far, and neither of them returned to the control room. The rest of the Marines gathered around. The poor light cast deep shadows on many of their faces, but Reyes knew they were all still staring at her, even if the darkness masked their looks.

Maybe the WO picked up on it, maybe not; either way, he broke the tension when he spoke. "Julius, how long do we have left before the *Crimson Destroyer* shows up?"

The tablet lit Julius' face. "Fifty minutes, sir, if this timer's still correct."

"We have to assume it is. We've got nothing else to go on. So that's fifty minutes to find the others and get to the escape pods. Whatever happens, we don't split up again, okay? If we stay together as a team, we can get out of here. Watch each other's backs, and if we hear another one of our own in trouble, we either all go together, or we don't go at all. One Marine's life isn't worth the lives of the group. You understand?"

The murmurs from many of the Marines confirmed they did.

"Right," he continued, "if we work together, we're going to get off this ship. Stay vigilant, and don't make any rash decisions. The heat scanners showed there were no living creatures on board, but something's clearly going on. Until we know what it is, I don't want any guesses. Speculation and paranoia won't help us here. If we focus on the basics and take it one step at a time, we'll be fine. The first thing we need to do is access the other sections of this ship. If we do that, then we can get to the escape pods so the *Crimson Destroyer* can pick us up. Hopefully we'll find the others on the way."

# CHAPTER 31

The WO led the line of Marines as they jogged down the dark corridor—blasters at the ready—towards the sports hall and the door to the second section of the ship. Where Reyes usually stayed close to her dad, she now held back. While running over the uneven surface, she watched her own struggles in the Marines in front of her, whose feet turned and slipped as they negotiated the treacherous floor. Their priority was to get to the escape pods. Once they'd secured their way off *The Faradis*, they could look for Patel and Grady—hopefully, they were still alive. If they found the corpses of Crouch and Lombardo, it would be a bonus, but none of them were going to risk their life or chance of escape for the sake of a dead body.

At first it had been strange for Reyes, but she'd now grown used to Chan running beside her. Chan had been so put out by Reyes questioning her professionalism she'd gone too far the other way. It felt like she'd taken it upon herself to be Reyes' own personal bodyguard.

All the Marines ran two abreast, save for Simpson, who took up the rear on her own. Not that it mattered, all thirteen of them were so close together they had each other's backs should anything happen.

Julius ran next to the WO at the head of the line. She had the tablet in her hand. It had proven damn near useless so far. They couldn't access any satellites with it, but at least it had helped reset their comms, and it had a schematic of *The Faradis* on it—albeit a poorly detailed one that told them nothing of the two extra sections.

Before they'd set off, the warrant officer told them they could only speak if they had something urgent to say. They didn't need all of them expressing how they felt. Their situation was FUBAR; discussing it wouldn't change that. He'd speak if he had to; otherwise, they needed to keep the channel clear.

They passed the dry food stores and then the briefing room. As they drew closer to the sports hall, Reyes' stomach sank. Crouch and Grady had been there when they were last in contact with them on the radio. Anxiety and guilt twisted through her. She and Chan should have saved them. And how had Crouch's corpse vanished into thin air? If her hands weren't wet with his blood at the time, she would have questioned her sanity.

The WO reached the end of the corridor and stopped—the door to the sports hall on his right, the entrance to section two of the ship on his left. He linked his fingers behind his head and pulled in deep breaths. It served as another reminder to Reyes of her dad's aging. The old dog didn't have the lung capacity he used to.

Once he'd recovered and the rest of the Marines gathered around, he looked straight at Reyes. The malice of only a few minutes ago had gone. "This is where you lost contact with Grady and Crouch?"

"Yep. We were talking to them from the opposite corridor on the radio while we both entered the room through our respective doors. But the second we stepped into the place, the radio cut off and we couldn't see them." As she said the words, her throat tightened and her pulse pounded through her skull. The dark and traumatised walls with their glossy red glow felt like they were closing in around her.

The WO pointed at the door to the second section. "Do you think something came through there and grabbed them?"

"I don't know what to think anymore. I mean, it's possible, but they tested the door while we were still in contact with them. They said it wouldn't open. Besides, nothing showed up on the scanners, right?"

"I think it's safe to assume we can't trust what we saw on the scanners." He then raised his voice to address all of them. "That doesn't mean I'm asking for speculation on our current situation. Just that we need to look outside of what we knew before we got on here."

"But I thought we had some of the best tech in the galaxy?" Austin said.

This time Julius spoke up. "We do. We can even detect beings using zinconium to shield their presence."

Both Austin and the warrant officer said it at the same time. "Zinconium?"

"It's a metal that blinds most scanners. So if you wanted to avoid being detected, nine times out of ten, hiding behind a shield of zinconium would do it. It's one of the galaxy's best kept secrets, which is why so few scan for it. But we do." Julius fell quiet for a moment, her eyes widening before she said, "Maybe the ship's sentient?"

The warrant officer's response came as a loud bark, making Julius jump away from him. "What?!"

A shrug of her wide shoulders, sweat glistened on Julius' brow, the red glow catching her sheen. "It's just a thought. This ship's like nothing we've seen before, so why rule out sentience?"

After watching Julius for a few seconds, he turned to the rest of them. "Okay"—his gruff tones bounced off the hard and dark walls—"we don't know how we're losing Marines on this cursed ship, and of course we all want to try to guess. I think we need to expect to find something living on here. Although speculation, it's the most rational explanation for what's been happening, and it's what we're going to stick with unless we get better evidence." He didn't give anyone else a chance to offer their theories. Instead, he said to Julius while nodding at the door with the number two above it, "Can you get us in there? We have to find the escape pods, wherever they are."

Sometimes it paid off to do the most obvious thing. As Reyes watched Julius walk up to the door and press the button, she almost commented, but she didn't have to because Austin called from behind her, "I bet you're glad you brought a techie on board, eh, sir?"

The grizzled vet glared at him.

"Sorry," Austin said. "When I get nervous, I tell jokes."

"*Bad* jokes," he replied.

Austin nodded and looked at the floor. "Bad jokes."

The WO returned his attention to Julius. The bright glow from the tablet stood out in the gloomy red as she waved it around. "Unless we can get this thing talking to some nearby satellites, I can't hack *anything* on this ship. It's no more than an expensive torch, and a poor one at that."

Silence swelled around them. The warrant officer stared at the door as if his intense focus would somehow open it. He then returned his attention to Julius. "How long do we have until the *Crimson Destroyer* gets here?"

The screen on the tablet glowed again at Julius' touch. "I suppose it's a half-decent timer too. We just need to hope it's giving us a true reading." When she met the WO's stare, she returned her focus to the backlit screen. "Forty-five minutes."

After grunting at her, he slammed his palm against the button on the door to the sports hall. Reyes and Chan—who stood the closest to it—jumped away from the loud sound. A moment's eye contact with her dad, Reyes then turned to watch the door reveal the large and empty room beyond.

Despite being the closest to it, Reyes waited for her dad to enter the sports hall first before she followed in after him.

The same red glow in the sparse arena, Reyes saw it looked like it had when she'd been in there last. She turned to her dad. "As you can see, if you walk from one side of this room to the other, it's quite hard to miss someone coming from the opposite direction. If Crouch and Grady had come in here at the same time as us—which is what they said they were doing—we would have seen them. Even with the poor lighting."

A brilliant white glow then filled the room. For the second time since they'd boarded the ship, the red emergency lights were replaced with the bright white glare of LED bulbs. So bright, they blinded Reyes like they had the first time around.

While rubbing her eyes, Reyes heard a loud *shoom* followed by a deep *boom* that ran a shock through the soles of her boots. She stared in the direction of the noise, but couldn't see anything.

Before Reyes regained her sight, she heard the screams. Several Marines were still out in the corridor. She knew what had happened, and as her sight returned, the closed door between them and those on the other side confirmed it.

Although the warrant officer hit the button to open them again, Reyes saw in his body language that he already knew. They had no hope of getting to the others through that way.

The Marines in the corridor continued to shout and scream. Their words were indecipherable through the cacophony of their combined panic. The sound of laser fire pulsed for the briefest of moments; then everything fell quiet.

Only seven of them had made it into the sports hall: Reyes, Chan, the WO, Julius, Holmes, Hicks, and Niamura. When the warrant officer looked at them all, his face pale in the bright glare, he said, "We have to go around. If they're still out there, we have to get to them ASAP!"

# CHAPTER 32

As the fastest of those remaining, and the fastest of those who'd boarded the ship—not that Reyes would admit that to her—Chan set off towards the door at the opposite side of the sports hall. A flatter floor than any other part of *The Faradis* they'd seen so far, it allowed Reyes to sprint after her.

Although the closest to Chan, Reyes was still over ten metres away from her by the time she reached the exit and slammed her hand against the button. The doors opened.

Reyes' apprehension far outweighed her relief, yet the very slight release of tension to see something go their way unsettled her stride as she closed down on Chan.

Where they'd simply charged through the doorways previously, this time Chan stepped halfway through and pressed her back against the door to prevent it from closing.

A second after Reyes burst into the dark corridor on the other side, the rest of those remaining followed her. When they were all through, Chan stepped aside, the door closing as soon as she allowed it to.

Close to the button to reopen it, Reyes pressed it out of curiosity. The doors didn't move.

The remaining Marines breathed heavily while staring at it.

Sweat beaded Holmes' dark skin. He too pressed the button with no luck. "What the hell's going on with this ship? It's like it's playing games with us."

Reyes saw Julius and the WO share a look, but she knew her dad wouldn't accept sentience as an option.

Holmes added, "It's opening and closing the doors it either wants us to go through or doesn't. I can't help feeling like we've got no control here."

"Without working scanners," the warrant officer said and threw a hopeful look at Julius as if she might tell him they were back online—she shook her head—"we don't know anything for sure. It's possible we're on the unlucky end of this ship malfunctioning and all these events are entirely random. Now, come on, we need to get to the other corridor."

In the few seconds they'd spent talking, Reyes stepped towards the next door. Just before they set off, she tested it.

The *whoosh* of the opening door silenced the rest of them, all of them turning to look at the corridor that hadn't been available to them until that moment. So dark, Reyes couldn't see any farther than a few metres into it. The floor lay as flat as the one in the sports hall.

"What do we do now?" Reyes said, raising her torch and shining it into the shadows. "This door might be locked when we come to it again."

While staring at it, the WO scratched his head. "We have six Marines back there."

Hicks shrugged. "But what if they've already gone? Every other time we've been separated from someone, they've vanished."

Had anyone else said it, the warrant officer might have listened to them, but Hicks had always been the first to panic in training. Anything he said had the underlying motivation of self-preservation. Even if he said something that made sense, the fact it came from him undermined the validity of it. The WO shook his head. "We're not leaving *anyone* behind. Besides, there are six of them. They should be able to survive against whatever's doing this to us."

Despite his words, Reyes saw the wobble in the warrant officer's resolve. When she looked at the others, she saw the same doubt on their faces.

"Damn it!" he said while running a hand through his hair. "We *need* to go to the others. We can't give up on them." It sounded like he wanted to convince himself as much as he did them.

"But this door might not open again," Chan said. Her words—unlike Hicks'—gave the others permission to back her up, all of them nodding.

The glow of Julius turning on the tablet took Reyes' attention away from her dad. They were running out of time.

"I'll stay," Holmes said, moving towards the door, straddling the doorway, and pressing his back to it so it couldn't close. "I'll keep it open and wait for you to come back."

A moment's pause while he stared at Holmes, the WO said, "We can't leave you on your own."

Niamura stepped towards the door. "I'll wait with him."

Not his usual frown, he appeared concerned rather than furious as he looked between Niamura and Holmes. "You sure?"

Both of them nodded before Niamura said, "Now go. Get the others and bring them back with you."

"We'll be as quick as we can." The warrant officer then set off up the corridor in the opposite direction to the open door.

Although she knew they'd find dead Marines at best when they got to the corridor on the other side, Reyes followed with the rest of the group. If there was a chance to save them, they had to try. Now only five of them left, even the group they were trying to save outnumbered them. Holmes and Niamura had best be there when they returned.

# CHAPTER 33

The WO led the way this time, his heavy stomp charging up the now brightly lit corridor. Although, how long it would stay brightly lit was anyone's guess. Also, Reyes found it no easier going for having better vision. If anything, it made it worse. She preferred it when she couldn't see how easily she could trip and fall.

The doors to the briefing room were the closest, so the warrant officer headed for them first. When he pressed the button, they parted with the now all too familiar *whoosh.* The ship obviously wanted them to go this way. To shake the thought of sentience from her mind, Reyes said, "Maybe it has something to do with the part of space we're in. You heard the *Crimson Destroyer*; they said it's a mess around here."

It took for her dad to look at her to show Reyes she'd had half the conversation in her head. "*The Faradis,*" she said. "It might be unpredictable because of the area we're in. Doors opening and closing, lights going on and off, radios not working—it's all electrically operated, so I wonder what the atmosphere's like outside."

The warrant officer stood in the doorway to give Reyes and

the others access to the briefing room. "How many times? I'm not interested in speculation."

The wrong place and time for the argument, Reyes stepped towards the open doors. Before she entered, she looked back down the corridor at Holmes and Niamura and muttered to herself, "I hope to see you both very soon." When she moved through the doorway, she brushed against the WO's wide frame.

Something about her dad as she passed him struck Reyes as odd. He looked unusually pallid. What had he seen? While she studied him, she stepped back to give the other Marines the space to enter the room. As each one came in, Hicks, Julius, and Chan, each one of them lost the colour in their face.

When Reyes turned to look in the same direction as the rest of them, she damn near pissed herself. The room itself had nothing to it. It looked like a wider corridor. The same seared flesh aesthetic warped the black metal on the floor, walls, and ceiling. It wasn't the design of the room that had shaken everyone up; it was what they'd all seen at the other end of it. A look as if to appeal to the others, she found all of them returning her focus. The same expression sat on all of their faces. No chance! As the first to enter the room, she had to lead them across it. It would have been the same for anyone in her position.

Reyes' heavy legs felt like they wouldn't work when she looked at it again. Directly opposite them, covering the door on the other side of the room, was a strung up and half-skinned Grady. His limbs were pinned to the wall surrounding the door. Blood ran from where he'd had what looked to be industrial rivets driven through his wrists and ankles. A fifth one had been fired through his forehead, evidenced by the halo of brain matter on the wall behind him. Whatever had done it to him had also opened him up like a frog in a classroom science experiment. A surgical cut down his front, his skin had been splayed wide and tacked to the wall too, revealing his muscles, skeleton, and internal organs.

The bright glow of the place lit him up as if he had a spotlight focused on him.

The bark of Julius' heave filled the room before the tall woman bent over double and threw up on the metal floor. When Reyes smelled her sick—added to the sight of the strung-up Grady—her body temperature rose, sweat lifting on her palms and forehead like she might vomit too.

Reyes jumped fully off the floor when the WO shouted, "Grady's dead. I know it doesn't look pretty, but he's *gone*. There might be others in the corridor outside that we can save." Not even he could hide the doubt in his tone.

The doors closed the second he stepped away from them. He walked over to Reyes and shoved her towards Grady's corpse. Although she stumbled across the uneven floor, it helped her find her legs, and she broke into a run. As the first into the room, she had to lead them across it.

As much as Reyes didn't want to look at the splayed Grady, her attention couldn't go anywhere but. When she reached the glistening corpse, she stepped in the pool of blood on the floor and leaned her face close to his exposed chest so she could reach around his body and press the button to open the doors behind him. As she pulled back, she hoped for the first time since being on *The Faradis* that the doors wouldn't open. When they did, she paused for a second before pulling in a deep breath, her stomach flipping as the rich metallic smell of Grady smothered her.

Every part of Reyes' being told her to stay put, but if she didn't move, Chan wouldn't ever let her live it down. The WO would tear her a new one too. Her old man's wrath she could cope with, but she had a duty to do this. She dropped down onto her hands and knees—her palms and trousers getting soaked with Grady's blood—and crawled through his spread legs. Before she'd reached the other side, a loud *clunk* ran through the ship and the bright white glare yielded once again to the warm and sinister glow of the red emergency lighting.

Through to the other side, Reyes got to her feet and pressed her back against one of the doors to prevent it from closing. She looked out into the corridor where the Marines they'd come to rescue should be. It might have been poorly lit, but surely she would have seen their shadows if they were still there.

Chan first, Julius next, and then Hicks—all three of them crawled through Grady's legs, and all three of them winced and heaved from the experience. As the last of them to come through, the warrant officer poked his head between Grady's legs. At that moment, Reyes' feet slipped on the bloody floor as the door at her back pressed against her when it tried to close.

Reyes lifted her right leg and pushed against the door on the other side. But they pushed too hard. One of them hurt her spine while the other one folded her leg up as if her muscles were useless. She winced and spoke with a gasp. "Help. The doors are closing, and I can't hold them on my own."

The WO pulled back into the briefing room and stood up again while Julius and Chan came to Reyes' aid. Even against all three of them, the strength of the doors was winning. Although slowed down, the gap continued to close.

Julius gritted her teeth with the effort of holding the door, and spoke to the warrant officer through them. "You have to come now if you want to make it. I'm not sure how long we can hold it for. Either that or go back to the others and we'll meet you there."

No way would Reyes let that happen. No way could she lose sight of her dad. Not on this ship.

Thankfully he reached the same conclusion and kneeled down to attempt it again. But Reyes could feel he wouldn't make it; the doors were winning. "If you get caught in this door, it'll cut you in two."

Still on his knees, he shouted up at her, "What would you have me do, then? Give me solutions, not problems."

Although she'd already seen what she needed to do, it didn't stop Reyes wishing she had another way. "Chan, Julius, I need you to hold these doors. Hicks, get over here and help them."

Both Marines nodded and Hicks joined the struggle.

Reyes stared at Grady's back. The skin spread out to either side of him was thin like bat's wings. It went against every instinct in her body, but she didn't have time to dwell on it. Instead, she yelled and wrapped her hands around his bloody corpse. Her fingers sank into the soft and wet mess along his front, but as much as she wanted to let go, she clenched her jaw through it. She then tugged hard.

Several parts of Grady's body tore with the sound of ripping flesh, and Reyes fell out into the hallway with it. A loud *tonk* sounded from where Grady's head slammed against the black wall behind them. A spray of moisture ran across her face. She didn't want to know what part of his body had delivered the damp assault.

While kicking Grady's corpse away from her, Reyes watched her dad jump through the gap, a much quicker way than doing it on all fours. Chan, Julius, and Hicks pulled away too, the doors slamming shut like pincers with a loud *thoom* that shook the walls around them.

Reyes shuffled away from the mauled body while wiping her hands against her thighs. She used the back of her sleeve to rid her face of the moist spray.

No time to dwell on it, Reyes pointed in the direction of the sports hall. The corridor was still bathed in the glow of emergency lighting, but she could see well enough. As soon as she'd looked down there, she'd been able to see well enough; she simply didn't want to vocalise it. "They're not here."

"We gave them a chance," the WO said as he set off towards

the sports hall doors. "It's what we owe our brothers and sisters. We don't give up on anyone until we have to. We need to leave Grady's body here. If we get a chance to come back for it, we will. Now let's go and see what we can find in the third section of this ship." When he hit the button that controlled the doors to the sports hall—the ones that had prevented them from getting back to the Marines in the first place—they slid open as if they'd never been locked.

# CHAPTER 34

R eyes led the way through the sports hall, the other Marines moving in time with her, their feet slamming down in stereo. Now she'd dealt with Grady's body, she could lead them into anything. At the doors to leave the room, she pressed the button and tensed in anticipation of them being locked. But they opened without resistance. Just before she stepped through, Hicks grabbed her arm, the sharp movement spiking her pulse.

"What?" Reyes said, her hard hiss running back across the room.

Something in Hicks' eyes had changed. They were wider than before. He'd always been one to lose his head quicker than the others, but his pale skin and glistening face showed he'd gone that little bit too far this time. While swiping his almost grey hair from his damp brow, he shook his head. "That just opened far too easily."

"This entire mission's been a steaming pile of shit; so what's your point, Hicks?"

"It might be a trap."

"*Everything's* been a trap. You ask me, if a door opens that we want to walk through, then we walk through it. We can't fight what hasn't yet happened, and I'm sure none of us need to be reminded to remain on high alert."

Hicks' mouth fell open, but he didn't reply.

When Reyes looked at the WO, he nodded at her.

Hicks yelped when the WO slapped a heavy hand on his shoulder. "This entire mission's gone to hell, Hicks." The deep rumble of his voice went the way of Reyes' hiss, back across the red-lit room in the direction they'd just come from. "We don't have any control, so the sooner you let go of that notion, the better. We don't know what's doing this, but we do know something is. Because we don't have any more intel than that, all we can do is keep moving and try to get to the escape pods. Do that and the *Crimson Destroyer* will find us. We can't think about things we haven't yet seen. We have no evidence for anything other than this ship has bent us over and is screwing us. We neither know how or why." He tapped his finger against his own temple. "You have every right to feel paranoid, but you don't have to let it win."

Not quite the pep talk Reyes would have given, but she watched Hicks nodding at the warrant officer. Good enough. When he flicked his head up to encourage her to go, she moved into the doorway and blocked it like she had when coming out of the briefing room. From her experience with Grady's body, she knew she didn't have the strength to stop it closing, but she could slow it down if it came to it.

Despite the poor lighting, Reyes clearly saw their current predicament when she looked at the door leading to the third section of the ship. Holmes and Niamura were nowhere to be seen. The door was closed. She'd been a fool to expect anything but that.

The WO stepped past Reyes and went for the door to the third section. *Bang!* He whacked the button to open it. Other than the snap of an echo running away from them, nothing happened. His broad shoulders sagged and he looked at the floor while shaking his head. "Shit!"

The other three filed out, Reyes turning to join the back of the line as she too stepped into the black metal corridor. Unlike the one leading from the briefing room, the door closed slowly. They all looked at the warrant officer, Hicks breathing more heavily than the rest of them. Not only did he breathe quicker, but he also sweated more than he had a few seconds ago. It now positively gushed from him. Reyes heard him emit the slightest whimper. His head had well and truly gone.

The sides of the WO's wide jaw swelled and relaxed several times before he looked up the dark corridor, back in the direction of the control room at the other end of the ship. Not necessarily hope, but something in his eyes lightened just a little. "What's the one room we've not searched properly?"

Although Reyes drew a blank, Julius said, "The dining hall."

"Exactly. It might show us nothing, but it's the only room we haven't properly checked out because we were too busy getting to the rest of the ship. I say we go back there in case it has anything to show us. Any objections?"

Silence.

"How long until the *Crimson Destroyer* gets here, Julius?"

The tall and wide Marine looked down at the bright tablet in her hand. "Just over thirty-five minutes, sir."

"Thirty-five minutes to figure out a way off this poxy ship. Come on." He barged through the Marines and broke into a jog in the direction of the canteen. They all followed him, Reyes taking up the rear.

CHAPTER 35

Because Reyes ran at the back of the line, she watched those in front enter the dining hall before her. The first she knew of it came when the others gasped and Hicks said, "What the hell?"

The reaction robbed Reyes of some of the strength in her legs, but she persevered and followed them in. They couldn't avoid whatever lay in wait for them. At least if they found some clues as to what they were facing, they'd be able to take positive action.

When Reyes saw the room, she froze. The strange tables that looked like they'd grown from the ground remained, except where they had been laden with piping hot food, they were now empty—every one of them. And not only empty, they shined brighter than before as if the black metal had been polished after the clean-up.

The WO shouldered his blaster, and the rest of them followed suit. They fanned out into an arrow formation, her dad at the front while Reyes moved out to the right wing. The place looked as empty as everywhere else.

Much slower steps than before, none of them spoke as they moved. Reyes pulled in a deep breath to slow her pulse and glanced across at Hicks to her left. Whatever they all felt, looking at his wild eyes told her he felt worse.

The last time Reyes had been in the dining hall, she hadn't seen the doorway on her right. Embedded in the twisted wall, it looked like it could lead to the control room next door. The top of the frame ended just before the dome of the ceiling began its arching curve. There must have been too much going on before, because even with the poor lighting from the red emergency glow, she could see it clearly. If they were going to find any more clues, they'd be on the other side of that door.

Other than the slow steps of their feet against the hard floor and Hicks' quickened breaths, they moved in silence. As they stalked across the room, searching left and right, they closed down on the door. Unlike all the others they'd come across on the ship, this one looked to be manually operated. Something they had control of at last.

When the warrant officer reached the wooden door, he kept a grip on his blaster, stood on one leg while lifting his right foot in the air, and slapped the handle down with the sole of his boot. The flimsy thing fell open into the room beyond, a creaking yawn from the hinges as it swung away from them. "At least we know we can bust that thing down should we need to get out again," the WO said before he walked through it.

Reyes remained at the back, passing through the doorway last. Like many industrial kitchens, the room beyond had ovens, hobs, and surface areas for preparing food. It only stood out as unique from the ones she'd seen before because it had been constructed from the same twisted black metal that made up the rest of *The Faradis*. Also, it looked immaculate. Brand new. Whatever chef cooked in there, they clearly had a handle on hygiene.

A large freezer sat at the back of the room. The door on the front stood both taller and wider than any they'd been through so far. "They must store a lot of food in there," Reyes said. "I'm guessing this ship is built for long journeys."

None of the others replied as they followed the warrant officer. One final look around, he pulled on the handle, the pop of a pressure seal and then cold mist falling out when he opened the door. The frigid rush raised gooseflesh on Reyes' skin when it surrounded her with its ghostly grip.

Before he entered, the WO kept a hold of the handle and paused. "I'm not sure we'll get back out again if we go in."

The others stared at the doorway, but none of them spoke until Reyes said, "Can you open it wider?"

Despite the slight twist of his features at her request, he obliged.

As Reyes had thought, the hinges were on the inside. "Stand back."

Several shots against the chrome joints and the door fell away from the freezer, slamming down on the metal floor with a loud *bang* that seemed to barrel through the entire ship.

They all paused in the aftermath of the noise, listening to see if something would respond to it. The WO finally said, "Well, that's one way of fixing the problem." He stepped into the freezer first. Chan, Hicks, and Julius all followed. One last look around the kitchen and Reyes followed him in too.

Where Reyes had felt cold outside the freezer, her entire body now locked tense against its frigid bite. She checked behind again in case anything had entered the kitchen. It still looked clear.

The freezer had a wide walkway through the centre of it, the white floor bright compared to the dark obsidian of the rest of *The Faradis*. Metal shelving ran from floor to ceiling on either side. Chrome shelving rather than the Gothic look that dominated so much of the ship. White frost dulled the silver shine. It looked like the many freezers Reyes had seen before. "I think we can assume humans have lived in here fairly recently. Either that, or a species with a diet so similar to ours it's uncanny."

The warrant officer looked closer at the food. "If only the tablet worked. We could do another scan for beings."

Before anyone could respond, Reyes heard a sound. Hicks went to speak, and she cut him off with an abrupt *shh*.

Their breath had been visible in the cold space, but Reyes saw they all now held it as they listened. Only faint, but she definitely heard it. In the widening of the eyes around her, she saw the others had heard it too.

"Ring-a-ring o'roses, a pocket full of posies, a-tishoo, a-tishoo, we all fall down."

# CHAPTER 36

Already covered in gooseflesh because of the cold freezer, Reyes shivered as she listened to the febrile, childish song. A ghostly whisper, she couldn't see where it came from. The looks on the others' faces suggested they couldn't work it out either.

The sharp sound of Chan clicking her fingers dragged Reyes' attention over to the small Marine. Her back to the rest of them, she pointed at the wall—a plain white dead end—and said, "It's coming from in there." Despite being the closest to it, she still stood about a metre away and didn't look like going any closer.

The warrant officer took control and stepped forward, bursting through Chan's most recent breath of condensation. He drove a hard knock against the back of the freezer, the thud amplified by the space behind it. The singing stopped.

"Patel?"

If they'd wanted the option of stealth, the WO's gruff approach had blown that out of the window. Although, if they'd wanted to be stealthy, Reyes shouldn't have shot the door from its hinges either. And who were they kidding? They couldn't hide from whatever controlled *The Faradis*. They were being well observed and had been since they'd set foot on the ship.

Other than ceasing his singing, Patel didn't respond to the warrant officer, who pressed his face to the barrier between them and shouted, "Stand back." He kicked at the wall. The false panel gave way with the tearing sound of wood and fell inwards, landing flat against the white floor with a loud *slap*.

They were all on edge, but Hicks took it to a whole new level, panting and gasping before he said, "*What the hell?*"

And he had every right to say it. Reyes' cold blood turned colder. Like she'd experienced many times since boarding *The Faradis*, she felt a heavy reluctance root her to the spot.

By knocking the false wall down, the WO had made the freezer twice the size. The same path ran down the centre of it, but at the new end, Patel sat strapped to a chair. Both his wrists were bound to the arms of the metal frame, his ankles to the two front legs. The frame itself had picked up the white fuzz of frosting, as had the ends of his eyelashes and the tips of the hair on his head. It seemed to take him a great effort to look up, his eyes rolling as he fought to stay conscious. He wore a mask of blood. His shirt had been ripped from his back—the cuffs and collar all that remained—and welts covered his body.

Down either side of the walkway, instead of shelves with food on, corpses hung from meat hooks. The ones closest to them swung from where the false wall had disturbed them when it fell. The corpses of humans, they'd all been tied up by their ankles. They'd all had their throats slit. Frozen pools of blood gathered beneath them. Dressed in the uniforms of Marines, Reyes finally said, "Shit. It looks like they're all here."

The WO stepped forward first, and Reyes followed behind him, passing Chan, who hadn't moved since identifying the false wall.

Reyes fought not to look at her fallen brothers and sisters.

They couldn't do anything for them now and, unlike Patel, at least they didn't have to suffer any longer.

Patel stuttered and shivered. His breaths manifested as small puffs of mist. He still wore his helmet, which must have been how they'd heard him on the radio. Although, with how his arms were tied, something else must have been pressing the button for him.

Were Patel not such a good friend, Reyes would have held back. Especially after what she'd had to do with Grady. As she and the WO drew closer to him, she stopped again. What she'd taken to be welts on his torso, she now saw as something more. After opening her mouth several times, she finally got the words out. "They've been eating him alive." Teeth marks ran around the edge of the chunks. It confirmed what she'd thought when first walking into the freezer. "And it looks like it's been done by humans."

While she spoke, her dad dropped to one knee and busied himself with untying Patel's ankles. Patel continued to shiver and shake, his eyes wild as if he had just the barest comprehension of them being in there with him.

"We need to get out of here," Hicks said. Of all of them, he stood the farthest back. "We need to get out of here *now!*"

It took for the warrant officer to release the first rope before Patel looked down at him, the delirium of only a few seconds ago giving way to laser-like focus. "No," he hissed, the WO jumping back and knocking into Reyes. "They'll come. They'll come." While shaking his head, he repeated himself. "They'll come."

The WO moved back towards Patel and continued to untie his bonds while Reyes put a hand on her friend's shoulder and leaned close to him. Despite his clear delirium, she had to try. "Who will come, Patel?"

He snapped out of it again and stared straight at her. "*Them.* They said to sing. As long as I keep singing, they won't do it anymore."

"Do *what?*"

Patel shouted so loudly, Reyes flinched away from him. "Eat me! They're fucking eating me alive. They said if I sing, they won't eat me, but they *lied.* They said they couldn't resist. They lied. Just kill me, Reyes, please." His tears magnified his brown eyes as he looked at her and whispered, "Kill me."

"What the hell?" Hicks said again.

"No." Reyes shook her head. "We're getting you out of here."

The warrant officer lifted Patel to his feet, and Reyes' heart sank to watch her friend fall forward. He slapped down against the floor like the false wall had. As he lay face down, she saw more holes in his torso. They'd also taken chunks from the back of his legs. The WO said, "What the …? They've chewed out his Achilles tendons."

It took for Chan to speak for Reyes to look back and see the others had stepped away. "Shit," she said. "He's screwed. How are we going to get him out of here? And how's he going to survive those injuries?"

The lucidity with which Patel had pleaded with Reyes had gone. He now shivered and twitched on the floor. A fish on a riverbank, he'd gone into shock. The kind of shock that preceded a painfully drawn-out death. As much as Reyes wanted to say she'd carry him and they'd get him some medical attention, she didn't. "You're right." She looked at Chan while drawing her blaster. One of the others would have done it, but she owed him this. "This is the only thing I can offer you now, brother." She paused, her hand shaking and her trigger finger weak as the tracks of her tears turned frigid. She wanted someone to tell her to stop, but none of them did. A gulp against the painful lump in her throat, she said, "I'll see you on the other side."

Reyes loosed a blast into the back of his head. The top of his skull and brain matter exploded away from him, and blood grew as an ever-expanding pool on the white floor.

Although she felt the others staring at her, Reyes didn't look up. Instead, she said a silent prayer for her friend. She'd done it for him. She'd given him the peace and escape he needed. May he rest now and know he was loved.

It took for Reyes to look up to see her dad staring at her. Tears covered his blue eyes. Sad, sure, but something else sat in the gaze. He bowed at her. "You're a force, my girl."

Reyes drew a breath to reply. Maybe now she could have the conversation she'd wanted to have with him for years. If time had shown her anything, it was that the moment would never be *right.* "Dad?"

The moniker clearly threw him off. It wasn't something she called him in front of the others.

But just as Reyes opened her mouth to continue, Julius said, "Um … I think I've just found out what we're up against."

# CHAPTER 37

J ulius had been examining the dead and strung-up Marines and stepped out from between two of them. Reyes had done her best not to focus on them, and she didn't try to work out who the two closest to Julius were now. They were already dead, so there seemed little point in giving them much more of her attention. However, the longer she spent in the frigid space, the harder she found them to avoid.

Only when Julius fully emerged did Reyes see why she'd called their attention to her. In her right hand, she had what looked like the skin of a lizard. It was big enough for her to wear as a shawl, and clearly weighed a lot because her large bicep bulged under the strain of it. She paused for a few seconds as if making sure she had the focus of them all on her.

"Archows," Julius finally said. When no one spoke, she elaborated. "They're lizard creatures that live in the frosty mountains of Aye-ow-ey. They're the only things that live up there because they're the only creatures that can. For eight months of the year, they eat the roots and plants that grow there. By the end of the feeding season, they can barely move they're so fat. For the other seven months, the temperatures drop so low, the place becomes uninhabitable. Instead of leaving, they let the harsh weather freeze them. Their bodies take on the cold and shut down until they're as good as dead. It's like a cryogenic sleep. When their warm season comes around, they thaw out and reanimate."

Maybe Reyes should have waited, but she spoke before she'd thought about it. "I'm struggling to make the connection between them and what's happening here. You say they eat plants, so that makes them herbivores, right?"

"Right," Julius said, "but the Archows are dead. Whatever creatures are on this ship—"

"Humans," Reyes said, casting a glance down at Patel's half-eaten body by her feet.

"I'm sure you're right because the lizard skins are the correct size for humans, and the food in the canteen looked like something humans would eat. But whatever species they are, I think they use the Archows' skins as shawls. The freezer and the Archows' skin go cold enough to disguise them to heat sensors."

"The skins go that cold?" the WO said.

Julius nodded. "I think we can also assume there are no more than thirteen of them because there are only thirteen suits."

The warrant officer shrugged. "Unless they have more freezers on board."

Another nod, Julius said, "That's true."

The WO took that moment to clear his throat with a gruff cough. It released an explosion of mist in the cold space. He gripped his rifle with both hands, pausing for a moment to look at Crouch upside down, his innards exposed and hanging from his body just like Reyes had seen in the corridor. "Well, we now have evidence that gives us a good idea of what we're facing. And sure, we're in their domain, but we can beat humans if we come across them."

A sound then rang out in the dining hall. A metal cup or plate being dropped, it made a tinkling noise as it hit the ground several times. They all turned around to look through the hole where the door had been. Hicks stepped backwards into the warrant officer, who shoved him towards the freezer's exit. "Get a spine, man."

Although Hicks shook, he nodded and stepped forward a pace. "But what if it's a trap?"

"Weren't you listening?" Reyes said. "This entire ship's a trap." She just wanted out of the damn freezer. Everywhere she looked, she saw the blue face of someone she cared about. The blue face or the ever-expanding crimson pool of Patel's blood.

When Hicks didn't respond, the WO said, "How long do we have until the *Crimson Destroyer* shows up, Julius?"

The mixture of cold and shock seemed to be getting to all of them. Reyes watched the tablet shake in Julius' hands as she looked at it. "Twenty-five minutes."

"Right, let's get off this damn ship, then. If we meet any other people on the way, we blow their fucking heads off, right?" The warrant officer then barged through Hicks and Chan and led the charge out of the freezer.

# CHAPTER 38

Reyes took up the rear again as they moved from the freezer, through the still-immaculate kitchen, and into the dining hall beyond. The second he entered the large domed space, the sound of an alarm tore through the ship. A voluminous and angry quack, the lights around them flashed in time with the noise, from bright white LED to blood red. The shadows brought to life by the alternating illumination made it seem like the ship changed shape with the pulse, the floors and walls shifting one way and then the other.

The optical illusion made Reyes even more cautious as she ran over the uneven floor. When she entered the dining hall, she had the butt of her blaster pressed into her shoulder. The others had stopped in the middle of the space and also had their weapons ready. They were all taking in the room, the lights altering their appearance, twisting their features with the deep shadows like they did everything else in there. The tables and stools hadn't moved—they looked to be a permanent feature in the hellish space—but the banquet had been re-laid. She wasn't close enough to see exactly what food had been put out.

It took for Reyes to look up to see why the others had stopped.

Spikes protruded from the ground around the edge of the room. They were spaced evenly—a gap of about two metres between each—and ran an entire ring around them. There looked to be about thirty in total. All the poles were made from the same black metal as the rest of the ship. Each one had the decapitated head of a human stuck on top of it.

Hicks made a retching sound before he bent over double and vomited on the floor. The rich, acidic tang of it added to Reyes' already churning stomach.

While wiping his mouth with the back of his sleeve, Hicks stood up straight again and said, "What the hell's happening? What are they doing to us?"

As much as she'd wanted to avoid looking at them like she'd avoided looking at the corpses in the freezer, when Reyes glanced across the room, one of the faces stood out to her. Austin, he stared back from one of the spikes. The bright glow and then deep drop in the light animated him, and it took a few seconds for Reyes to confirm his features weren't moving, despite there being no body attached to his head. His mouth hung wide, his tongue forced from it. He stared at Reyes through listless eyes, blood still dribbling from where his neck had been severed from his body.

Reyes stepped closer to the table and looked down. When she saw what had been laid out, she shook, and it took her a few seconds to get her words. "Are they what I think they are?"

Hicks came back quicker than the others. "They're body parts. Fingers, toes …"

When he stopped, Reyes looked up at him to see why. He now stared at the wall. Scrawled on it, only visible in the bright light, were words written in blood. The glare of the LED bounced off the glistening script. The blood still fresh, it read *WELCOME TO HELL.*

While Hicks whimpered, the WO shouted over the alarm, "As shocking as this is, they've not confronted us yet. Sure, it's horrible to look at, but they're trying to turn our own fear against us. They're cowards." He then shouted even louder, "Show yourselves!"

They all looked around as if his words would have the same effect on their captors as it had on them. Of course they didn't show themselves; why would they? They were in control, and no amount of the WO's wrath would change that.

The warrant officer then moved towards one of the doors out of there, the rest of the survivors following him. When he pressed the button, it didn't open. Not that Reyes expected it to.

They moved at a jog to the other exit. The WO had to shove Austin's head to one side to press the button next to the door. It remained closed. "Damn it. Get back into the centre of the room. It's the best position to defend from. How long do we have left, Julius?"

"Twenty-two minutes."

"We're screwed," Hicks said, shouting over the incessant alarm. "We're sitting ducks."

When they reached the middle of the room, Reyes looked down to make sure she didn't step in Hicks' vomit. Regardless of all the blood she'd already trodden in—and even crawled through —she couldn't cope with sick. The same alternating lights from red to white, the white helped her see the glistening pile like it had helped her see Austin's head and the writing on the wall. But it showed her something else too.

Her stomach doing backflips, Reyes hunched down closer to the sick and reached for the piece of the floor Hicks' had vomited on. Because the ship had been so dark for so much of their time on there, they'd had no way of seeing it until now. She slid her fingers into the grate, the slick feel of Hicks' bile against her touch. While wrapping a tight grip around it, she pulled. A section the size of a manhole cover came free.

Reyes threw the cover away from her with a clang before she

looked up to see the others watching. "Sorry about the noise, but I think I've just found out how they get through this place without us seeing them."

Normally the warrant officer would go into the hole first as the leader, but at his age, he didn't have the dexterity to head up a team through a rat run. Before they could have the discussion, Reyes sat down—the seat of her trousers turning wet with Hicks' puke—and slid into the dark hole, her nose flashing past the acrid stench of vomit.

After flicking on the torch on the end of her gun, she pointed it one way and then the other. The tunnel looked clear. At least, what she could see of the tunnel looked clear, and because they now had a floor between them and the lighting, her torch was much more effective than it had been above. "It looks okay," she called up at the others.

While straining her tired eyes to see as best as she could, she said, "I think this might be our way out of here."

# CHAPTER 39

Despite having a view much farther ahead now they were in the tunnels, Reyes still couldn't see the end of the section they were currently in. She headed up the team—Julius at the back—and they pushed on into the darkness, the occasional splash of light coming down through the grates as they passed beneath them. The grates were so few in number there was no way she would have noticed them were it not for Hicks vomiting where he had. A glance at his still-pallid complexion, he wore a glazed look that suggested his mind had gone elsewhere.

They moved at a slow pace, no one speaking as they walked down the tight tunnel in single file. The organic and tormented twist of the walls, floors, and ceilings above them hadn't carried down to where they were. It looked more like a maintenance corridor, every surface flush, right angles where the walls met the floor and ceiling. It was functional; aesthetics be damned. Reyes would take functional any day—especially over the aesthetics above. The risk of falling might have been seriously reduced, but they still needed to go slowly so they remained as quiet as possible. Should the cannibals choose to confront them down there, they needed to hear them coming. The loud quack of the alarm above made that much trickier.

When they came to the first fork in the tunnel, Reyes stopped. She shone her torch down each option in case the obvious choice revealed itself. It didn't. The WO stood in the middle of the five, so she turned to him, shrugged, and showed him the two options by shining her torch down them again. He motioned for her to go right.

Surely a guess, but no one else offered anything better, so Reyes took the right fork and plunged on into the darkness. Every urge told her to run, but the second they did, they'd lose any hope of hearing their enemy.

After a few metres, the tunnel opened slightly wider. Although Reyes looked up through one of the grates, she couldn't see anything other than the alternating glow of the lights. But she knew they were now beneath the main corridor down the right side of the ship. The side that led to the door with the number three above it. She moved off again, heading for it and hoping it would give them a way through.

A few metres farther down, Reyes stopped when something caught her eye. She pointed her torch up at the ceiling to show the others; it lit up a switch of some sort.

When Julius shoved forward to see what she pointed at, the hench Marine said, "They're manual overrides. I suppose we now know how they opened and closed doors at their will, even with the main control computer down."

"That makes me feel better," Chan said.

Julius shrugged. "How's that?"

"I didn't want to say it, but since you shot the control computer, I was worried they might be able to get *The Faradis* to make the jump to hyperspace. I mean, they were still controlling it somehow. I thought they might be using a backup computer to lock the doors and mess with the lights. Now we know they did it manually, I feel more confident that the hyperdrive is definitely down. I can't see them cranking that thing up by hand."

Although Julius nodded, she didn't reply.

The switch sat in the top of a doorway that led through to a larger space beyond. Reyes had been right to think they were beneath one of the main corridors, because the layout of the tunnel mirrored what they'd seen above. From the look of things, they were currently beneath the door to the control room; the space on the other side of the doorway was an empty representation of the room they'd been in earlier. If they looked hard enough, they'd probably find the hatch the cannibals had used to drag Lombardo's corpse through. "Let's keep moving," she said, leading them off down the tunnel again.

The library next, Reyes stopped and shone her torch into the space.

"What is it?" Julius said.

"When I was in the library, the shelves changed around." She highlighted the runners in the ceiling of the room beyond. "I just wanted to make sense of how they did it." She shuddered. "It's even more freaky to think about them scurrying beneath me while I was up there on my own." It wouldn't do to think on it too much, so she set off again.

They passed the dry food store, and just before they got to the briefing room, Julius slapped a hand on Reyes' shoulder that made her jump. She'd chosen to remain behind her, and Chan had now taken up the rear. As long as Hicks didn't try to put in a shift back there, they'd be covered. He didn't have it in him to watch their backs in his current state. She then looked up to where Julius shone her torch on the ceiling above them.

"I've seen these devices before," Julius said, addressing the WO more than any of them. "They're quite common, actually."

He scowled at her and he shrugged aggressively. "*Well,* what are they?"

"Miniature EMPs."

The blank look on his face suggested he was losing his patience.

"This is what screwed with the radios and all of our timers. Another one of their tricks to disorientate and divide us."

A moment to listen for the sounds of approaching steps, Reyes then looked at her dad and saw him staring back at her. His eyes widened as if to tell her to get moving. She set off again for the third section.

They reached the end of the tunnel and the start of section three without incident. Like they'd seen for every other doorway they'd come to, the doors only existed on the floor above them. It left their way through to the third section completely clear.

Once they'd passed beneath the locked door, Julius said, "Hang on."

The glow of the tablet shone on her face as she stared down at it. "I think we can reach satellites from here." Several images flashed across the tablet as it downloaded new information from having gotten back online. When the images cleared, Julius showed the others the screen. It had a schematic of *The Faradis* on it. "For some reason, we still can't contact the *Crimson Destroyer*. It looks like our comms are blocked. But at least we know where the escape pods are. As long as we get to them in time, we're home free."

The WO leaned forward to get a better look at the screen.

Julius pointed at the image while explaining, "The pods are in the second section. Right at the very end. We should be able to pass beneath the sports hall and get to them without any problem now; if this side is anything to go by, that is. But there's something else I need to show you." This time Julius pointed at the end of the third section. The end of the corridor they were currently on.

"What's that?" the warrant officer said.

"The power source for the ship. If we go down there, we can manually overload it and turn *The Faradis* and all its crew to dust. The *Crimson Destroyer* doesn't have the firepower to take this ship down on its own."

"Damn hippies," the WO said.

Reyes saw both sides of it, but she leaned more to her dad's way of thinking. Too many lives had been lost in the galaxy, so firepower had been reduced on every vessel within the galactic union. They could still defend themselves, but they couldn't blow up something as large as *The Faradis* anymore. Only smugglers and pirates carried weapons of that magnitude now. It meant that when they truly needed to take something out, they couldn't. The decision had been taken away from them.

"And how long do we have left?" he said.

Julius switched screens to show a timer. "Fifteen minutes."

"That should be enough, right?"

"It's not a quick job, but I reckon I can rewire it in five, which should give us plenty of time to get to the pods after."

It seemed like madness to Reyes. "Let's just get to the escape pods. If we do that, we live to fight another day."

"You think we'll ever find this ship again?" the WO said. "We let it go now and it'll be trawling the galaxy so it can bait humans to slaughter for years to come. Above all else, we're *protectors*; we can't leave this ship to continue its reign of terror."

As much as Reyes hated the idea, she couldn't argue with him. Before she could speak again, he said, "But only Julius and I are going."

"What?" Both Reyes and Chan said it in unison. Hicks hadn't said much for quite some time. He'd been checked out since they'd seen the severed heads in the dining hall.

"There's no point in all of us going down there. You, Chan, and Hicks get over to the escape pods, and we'll stay in contact. Get the pods ready for us; we'll be there in time."

A quickened pulse forced rapid breaths from Reyes as she looked at her dad. "You promise?"

An involuntary twitch ran through his right cheek just below his eye. "Just be ready for us, yeah? Julius, will the radios work okay?"

Julius nodded. "As long as we're in these back two sections, then yes, they'll stay in range of one another and the EMPs won't reach us here." She pressed the talk button on the side of her helmet to demonstrate. "Can you all hear me?"

When Reyes looked back at her dad, her tears had turned him into a blur. "You come back to me, you hear?"

He opened his mouth to respond, but got cut off by the sound of laughter. It echoed through the tunnel and came at them from where they'd just been. As one, they raised their weapons and stared into the darkness.

# CHAPTER 40

Despite the main tunnel being wider than the one they'd first entered beneath the dining hall, it still only gave them the space to move two abreast. As Reyes walked into the darkness —Chan next to her and the others behind—she gulped, her throat both dry and tight. Her eyes stung from where she strained to see, the torch on the end of her blaster working better than it had above, but still not well enough to give her a clear line of sight. If only her view of the thing laughing was as crystal clear as its barrelling cackle. It sounded human, but the tempo of its erratic giggle beat to a rhythm she'd not heard another human make before—then again, she'd never met a cannibal before.

They closed down on the tittering sound until it swirled around them in the confined space, manic and unhinged.

When Chan fired her blaster, Reyes jumped aside, slamming into the wall on her left. She watched the green shot fly away from them before it hit something with an emerald explosion. The strobe gave them a momentary sight of what they faced: human, just like they'd already suspected.

Reyes listened to the body hit the ground and then silence. A moment later, the thing laughed again.

Now they'd taken the man down, Reyes pushed off from the wall and jogged towards him. Her gun raised, she stared down the barrel at the crumpled silhouette. Despite her bold approach, Chan was bolder, charging ahead of her at full tilt. Instead of keeping her focus on the laughing human, Reyes shifted her focus so she covered the small Marine's back instead.

Chan reached the man first and pointed her weapon and torch down at him. She then stamped on the blaster in his hand and dragged it behind her with the sole of her boot. The slide of metal over metal rushed across the floor as it came spinning towards Reyes.

Sweat glistened on the man's face as he looked up at his aggressor. Although Chan had clearly hit him and he held his stomach, his eyes were lit and his grin stretched wide with glee. As if to put the others at ease, Chan momentarily raised her torch to show the empty space behind him. If there were others, they were currently holding back.

After she'd moved a few steps closer, Reyes stopped again, and the WO walked into the back of her. What she'd assumed to be sweat on the fallen maniac's face, she now saw was blood. She also noticed he held onto something. At first it had been hard to make it out in the dark, but now she saw it all too clearly: a human leg.

The tittering cannibal waited for all of them to catch up before he threw a name badge down on the floor in front of them. As covered in blood as the man, the patch had *CROUCH* written on it. In between giggles, the man paused and fixed on Reyes. "I was watching you talk to him, you know?"

To reply to him would fuel his fire and stoke his ego. Instead, Reyes simply stared down at him, clenching and unclenching her jaw. The desire to kick him in the face twitched through the muscles in her right leg.

"Don't you remember?" the man said. "It was when you were

up in the hallway on your own. When he had his guts in his hands. Then he vanished." The man's eyes widened and he raised his right fist before blowing on it and showing her his empty palm. "Poof! I heard you, Reyes."

The use of her name made Reyes step forwards a pace, but her dad grabbed her shoulder to stop her going any farther.

The cannibal continued to watch her, mocking her by trying an approximation of her voice. "Where did he go? I don't understand." The man covered his mouth as if trying to hold back his laughter. His maniacal titter unsettled his delivery. "I was already chewing into him by then. I was tasting his juicy flesh while you were all above, discussing what to do next. Oh, it was hard not to laugh. The only way I could stop myself was by eating more and more of him."

Reyes didn't try to fight off her dad's restraint. She'd found her head again, so she remained where she stood. The cannibal wanted a reaction, but she wouldn't give it to him. Five blasters trained on him, he'd die when they decided, not because he'd goaded her into a reaction.

"You used thermal imaging to check the ship, right?" the man said.

Julius spoke before Reyes could. "We already know how you hid from us."

It took the man's attention to her. His eyes were swimming with either insanity or blood loss, Reyes couldn't tell. He laughed again. "It works every time."

"Why?" asked Hicks this time, the worst of all of them to be talking to the man. Already rattled, he didn't need to be wound any tighter.

The cannibal took another bite from Crouch's leg, blood seeping from it and coating his maw. When he pulled it down, he chewed the meat and shrugged. "Isn't it obvious? We've got to eat. I bet you thought the ship was haunted, didn't you? Most people do. Or they think it's sentient." He laughed. "Having our prey freaked out helps. A haunted ship that jumps into hyperspace whenever it wants to. Most of the place sealed off from the rest. Doors opening and closing seemingly at random. Or even worse: by design. You've gotten quite far. Farther than most. Although you won't last much longer."

The man seemed so unable to control his excitement, he shook. But instead of delivering the punch line, his expression changed into something Reyes hadn't yet seen nestled in the personification of horror before her. He was crying. Tears streamed from his eyes. Polar opposites, pleasure and pain in one expression. She'd heard that it sends a human insane to eat their own. But before she could dwell on it, she heard something else.

The swell of footsteps sounded out in the distance. They came towards them from behind the man—from the direction of the dining hall and control room. The others must have heard it too because all of them except Chan—who kept the man in front of them pinned down by aiming her blaster at him—raised their weapons.

The man laughed again. "I told you. Not long left."

"How many of you are there?" Hicks said, his voice rising as if mimicking the lunatic on the floor.

The cannibal laughed again. "That freezer you saw isn't the only one on this ship."

The swell of a stampede drew closer, the tight metal tunnel amplifying the mob's approach.

A shrill sound, the cannibal laughed with piercing alacrity. "I'm the canary. The already dead rabbit in a bear trap. The worm on the hook."

When Reyes looked behind her at her dad, he nodded, turned from the man and the stampede, and ran back in the direction they'd come from. Why stay and fight when they didn't have long left? They needed to reach the escape pods so they could get off the ship. Whatever happened, they couldn't miss the *Crimson Destroyer*.

Chan looked back at them and gave chase after putting a blast through the cannibal's forehead. But Reyes saw Hicks remain rooted to the spot.

The first blast from the pack behind burst from the darkness. Blue laser fire, Reyes saw it hit Hicks' left shoulder and spin him as a puff of blood rose from the impact.

Reyes stopped, making eye contact with Hicks before looking past him at the crowd. Hard to tell how many of them there were, the tight pack of the hallway only showed her the front-runners. There were enough to make the swell of their steps sound like a tsunami coming at them. Although she stopped, the WO, Chan, and Julius were still running away. They obviously hadn't seen Hicks.

Another blue blast crashed into the back of Hicks' leg, blowing his patella out and dropping him down onto his opposite knee. Even in the dark, Reyes saw the bloody mess it had made before she looked into his pained face, his mouth wide in a silent scream.

For the briefest moment, they stared at one another before Hicks motioned her away with a frantic wave of his hand. "Just go. You'll *die* trying to save me. We'll *both* die."

The urge to run coursed through her, but Reyes couldn't move. How could she leave him? The mob had drawn close enough for the vibration of their stampede to shake the floor beneath her feet.

"*Go!*" Hicks said. "Even if I could get away, I don't want to. I'm done. I'll hold them back."

A lump in her throat and her face buckling out of shape, Reyes tried to speak but simply mouthed *sorry* while shaking her head.

Just before Reyes turned away from Hicks, she saw a calmness in his stare. Peace. He showed her the grenade in his hand and managed the slightest of smiles before softening his tone. "Now go!"

Reyes turned and ran on the heels of the others, the tattoo of rapid blaster fire echoing behind her. It sounded like Hicks had started to shoot back.

Out of breath from the short sprint, Reyes caught up to the others at the point where the entrance to the sports hall met the entrance to the second section of the ship. "Hicks is down. He has a grenade and is holding them back for as long as he can."

After dipping a stern nod, the warrant officer said, "There was no saving him?"

"They blew his kneecap out. Besides, he didn't want to be saved."

He winced before saying, "You and Chan need to get the hell out of here."

"What?"

"Julius and I still need to stop this ship. We have to blow it up."

Tears itched Reyes' eyes. "How long is left before the *Crimson Destroyer* arrives?"

Julius showed her the tablet. The timer had just over ten minutes left. She then passed the device to Chan. "When we get off this ship, this will allow you to communicate with the *Crimson Destroyer*."

While looking between the tablet and her dad, Reyes said, "But Julius said it will take five minutes to overload the power source. At least."

The way her dad pressed his hand on Reyes' shoulder showed her she had no choice. "Just get to the escape pod and wait for us, okay? We're going to set this ship so it's ready to blow. We'll catch up to you after."

"Promise?"

When Chan pulled on Reyes' arm to try to drag her into the sports hall, Reyes shook her off and raised a clenched fist as she stared at the smaller Marine. For the first time since they'd met one another, Chan backed down. Unable to stop her tears, Reyes looked back at her dad. "Do you *promise* you'll make it back to us?"

"We'll get back to you. Now go!"

Julius then said, "The radios will work when you cross through into the second section on the other side. We'll stay in contact."

A loud explosion shook the floor beneath Reyes' feet, and a bright glow shone in the corridor where they'd just come from. A second later, a wave of heat crashed into them. Then they heard more footsteps. "Shit!" Reyes said. "He didn't get them all."

Chan tugged on Reyes for a second time. After a lingering look at her dad, Reyes nodded. "See you at the escape pod," she said before following Chan into the room beneath the sports hall.

# CHAPTER 41

R eyes could never catch Chan in training, so as they ran now, she could only look at her blurred view of the Marine's back. Her grief tightened her lungs, and her throat burned with the lump nestled in it. They had to get to the escape pod and prime it. She had to trust her dad and Julius could blow the ship up on their own. Whatever happened, they'd wait for them.

When Chan reached the door exiting the sports hall, she stopped and waited. Instead of stopping too, Reyes ran straight past her and continued into the second section. She passed into it as easily as they'd gone into the third. No doors. No uneven floor.

"Hey!" Chan called and ran after her.

But Reyes didn't answer, continuing at a jog down the corridor towards a darkness her torch struggled to penetrate.

Chan caught up to Reyes and pulled on her arm. It both halted and spun her around. She clenched her jaw and balled her fists. "I swear, if you touch me again, I'm going to knock every tooth out of your fucking mouth." Tears continued to burn her eyes, and her bottom lip twisted out of shape, but she wouldn't look away. If Chan tried it again, she'd knock her fucking head off.

The usual spark of conflict both rose and died in Chan's green stare. She looked from one of Reyes' eyes to the other and sighed, her frame slumping as she dropped her attention to the floor. "I'm sorry. Lead the way."

So geared up for the fight, Chan's response threw Reyes off, her tears gushing harder than ever.

"Your dad will make it," Chan said.

Another hot wave, Reyes lost the ability to speak and nodded instead.

"Come on," Chan said and set off up the dark corridor. They moved at a slower pace. They had the time. If only the same could be said for her dad and Julius.

The distant pulse of blaster fire stopped them both dead. Reyes pressed the microphone on the side of her helmet. "Dad? Are you okay?"

When his voice came back to her, he had to shout over the loud laser fire. "We're fine," he said, sounding strained as he ripped off more shots. "We're holding back the ones Hicks couldn't. There aren't many. Are you at the escape pods yet?"

"No."

"Well, get running and stop talking. Julius is making good progress here. Get a pod ready for us."

"Are you sure you don't want us to come back? We can attack them from behind."

"No, we've got this. We need to make sure an escape pod's ready for when we get there. Now *go!*"

It wouldn't take much to go back. If they surprised the cannibals by attacking them from behind, they could end the battle in seconds. But her dad had said no. She had to respect that.

"Come on," Chan said.

Instantly on the defensive, Reyes turned on her, her hackles raised.

Again, Chan kept her tone even. "Your dad said he had it

covered. We have to make sure we've prepped an escape pod for when they get to us. We need to be certain of making it to the *Crimson Destroyer*."

Reyes pushed through the reluctance in her leaden legs and set off again with Chan. Just a few steps later, they saw the end of the tunnel.

Rungs ran a vertical line up the wall on their left. Reyes shone her torch up at the ceiling to see a grate like the one they'd moved aside in the dining hall.

A flash of competition rose in Reyes, but she quickly let it die as she watched Chan climb the ladder. It really didn't matter who got there first. Besides, Chan probably had the clearer head and was in a better place to deal with whatever waited for them above.

Chan pushed the grate clear, a bright white glow shining a spotlight down on them. The alternating flash of red and white had gone. Reyes watched her move out of the way before she grabbed one of the cold metal rungs in front of her.

It dazzled Reyes to climb out through the hole and stand in the bright glare of the light reflecting off the glossy metal. It stung her already sore eyes, and it took a few seconds for her to regain her sight. The corridor had the same onyx gloss as the rest of the ship, but it looked like any normal corridor, much like the tunnels beneath them had. The twisted organic design had clearly been part of the disorientation of their prey, an effective part of it.

Chan—who'd had a few seconds longer to recover her sight—had already moved over to the escape pods. Exactly where Julius had said they'd be, she pressed the screen beside one of them. It had one word written across it in bold red letters on a black background: *ENGAGED*.

A press of the button on the side of her helmet, Reyes said, "All's good with the escape pod, WO. We're here waiting for you. We'll be ready to go the second you arrive."

# CHAPTER 42

Just over three minutes had passed, but it felt like longer … much longer. Reyes sat in the escape pod with Chan and looked around for what felt like the twentieth time already. Other than windows, a bench, a control panel, and a small airlock, the pod didn't have much to look at. Functional, it was a million light-years away from the ghastly design of the ship's main section.

"I'm sorry," Chan said, the first words spoken between them since they'd sat down.

Reyes clenched her jaw while staring at her.

"I've been an arsehole for the longest time."

"You have."

"I dunno. I've always been so angry and jealous."

But before Reyes could respond, the hiss of radio static stabbed into her ears. She straightened on the bench and pressed the microphone on the side of her helmet. "Dad?"

At first she only heard gunfire—a lot of it. While listening to it, she looked at Chan. The small Marine offered her a tight-lipped smile. She looked like she wanted to give Reyes hope but couldn't find it in herself. While she saw the gesture for what it was—and almost appreciated Chan's effort—she couldn't look at her any longer. She turned to the window behind her and gazed into the starry oblivion outside.

The WO finally spoke. It sounded like it had taken him that long to find his words. "There have been some complications."

Now she could see her reflection in the window, Reyes watched her face buckle. Her tight throat gripped onto her voice, strangling it when she said, "What?"

"We're not going to make it." It sounded like he had to fight to get his words out. Like he'd been injured. More gunfire called through the headset. "The good news is Julius has nearly set this ship to blow. She said you must only have a couple of minutes before the *Crimson Destroyer* gets to you. At the most. I'm going to hold them back while she finishes up and you'll be long gone before *The Faradis* explodes."

"We'll wait for you."

"Even if we could get back to you, it'll take us ten minutes, maybe more."

"We'll wait."

"The *Crimson*—" he paused as if fighting for breath "—*Destroyer* won't. It *can't*. It'll be there for three minutes. If you're not on it, you're dead. You need to launch the escape pod. We're done for. You're not."

"We'll wait."

A spike of anger flashed through his voice. "You're not listening to me. We're *screwed!* Both Julius and I have taken too many hits. We're hanging on here. Just. You need to recognise when something's a lost cause."

Hot tears ran down Reyes' cheeks. "Don't say that. You're *not* a lost cause. We have to try. There has to be a way."

After he'd let go of a hard sigh, he said, "Sometimes, a good Marine has to know when to quit. We've lost. Don't make it worse by letting me die knowing my daughter's gone too."

It took several seconds before Reyes said, "I love you, Daddy." When she felt Chan put a hand on her back, she leaned into it. Chan shifted closer and put her arm around her.

They both listened to her dad talk, his breathing laboured. "I've never been the best dad. Since Mum died, I've tried my hardest."

It took a few seconds of Reyes shaking her head before she found it in her to speak. "You've been great. You took a career break to raise me. You made sure I finished school with the love of a parent at my side. Don't you *dare* feel bad about how you dealt with it. You were *everything* I needed. You could have packed me off to boarding school with all the other military brats, but you saw the value of being there for me."

Several deep breaths, the sound of gunfire behind him, he said, "I watched you turn into a fine human being. There were conversations your mum should have had with you that I couldn't. You had to figure things out because I found them too awkward to talk about. Changing from a girl into a young woman is hard enough without having to do it alone."

"I had good friends. They helped. I feel guilty about you putting your career on hold."

"After Mum passed, my career became much less important. I would spend that time with you again in a heartbeat."

"Besides," Reyes said, pausing to catch her breath, a damp weight pushing down on her chest, "you were there. That was the most important thing. I was the only girl in my year who went shopping for a prom dress with her dad. That was special." She laughed in spite of herself. "You were so embarrassed in that shop, do you remember?"

As she listened to her dad cry on the other side, Reyes added, "That was about as uncomfortable as I've ever seen you."

Her dad pulled in a wet sniff and laughed. "I'm glad it gave you so much pleasure."

Reyes smiled through her tears and leaned back into Chan's tight hug.

"Look, sweetheart," he said, "you need to leave the Marines. It's a mug's game. I want you to go and see a being called Moses Deloitte. Tell him who you are, what's happened to me, and that it's time. He'll help you." After a moment—more gunfire ringing through the speakers—he said, "Julius reckons you now have about a minute before the *Crimson Destroyer* arrives. You need to get going. Know I'll be with you always."

Blinded by her tears, were Reyes not sitting down, she would have fallen down. Words seemed beyond her grasp, but she had to say it. The one thing she'd never been able to tell him. Not because of him, they just didn't have those kinds of conversations. "Dad, I'm—"

"I know," her dad said. "I've known since you were a kid."

"You *have?*"

"I could see you were never into boys like your friends."

"Why didn't you say something?"

"I wanted you to tell me when you were ready. I figured you'd do it when the time was right. Besides, it doesn't change anything. I love you, little squirrel."

He'd not called her that for the longest time. For the next few seconds, Reyes wept as she listened to her dad crying too.

"Now go," he said. "Don't you dare miss your ride out of here. Make my and Julius' efforts worth something."

Barely the strength to move, Reyes pulled away from Chan and turned to see her cheeks were soaked too, her eyes bloodshot. She then looked at the touch panel next to the escape pod's door. A green button sat in the centre of it that read *LAUNCH*. She reached for the panel and pressed the button as she said, "I love you, Daddy. So much."

# CHAPTER 43

The rush of the boosters shook the tiny escape pod as Reyes and Chan shot away from *The Faradis*. The vastness of space often gave a strange perspective to many things. To see the black ship from the outside made it look so small. So insignificant. Reyes looked at the section she knew her dad and Julius to be in, her eyes burning, her view blurred, her nose running. Even now, despite knowing she had none, she still clung onto the smallest amount of hope. Her dad would make it out. He always made it out.

Reyes gasped when a flash of light punched through the darkness. It came from where her dad and Julius were. The bright spark ignited a line of fire, which streaked up the vessel towards the middle section in a series of grand and brilliant explosions.

Seconds later, *The Faradis* burst into a swollen sphere of white heat that thrust the black metal vessel away from it in every direction. Reyes flinched to watch some of the large pieces fly at them, but they were already far enough away to be out of range of the worst of it.

For the entire time, Chan had sat beside Reyes and not spoken. She finally broke that, pointing at the screen on the wall.

"Good job we came out so close to the *Crimson Destroyer* arriving. If we'd left too early, we'd be screwed. There's only five minutes of oxygen remaining in this thing."

It took for Reyes to rub her eyes and squint at the control panel to see it better. She needed to keep her head. At least until they got on the *Crimson Destroyer*. "Only five minutes? How?"

"I'm guessing the cannibals drained as much as they could in case we escaped. The five minutes is the emergency backup. They wouldn't have been able to get that out of the tanks."

"But we only need one minute, right?"

Chan pressed the WO's tablet, the screen lighting up at her touch. She opened their connection to the *Crimson Destroyer* and said, "Chan Furi to *Crimson Destroyer*; come in, *Crimson Destroyer*."

The reply came back instantly. Still wound so tightly she felt like she'd snap, Reyes loosened a little to hear it. Her grief pushed to the back of her being, she'd only let it go when they were safe. "Chan Furi, this is the *Crimson Destroyer*. We're on our way and will be there at the agreed time. We now have your exact location."

"Thank you so much," Chan said, slumping where she sat and releasing a long sigh. "We'll see you in one minute."

"*One minute?*"

Any slight loosening of Reyes' muscles snapped tight again. She looked at Chan, whose face had lost all its colour. "*Not* one minute?"

"We're going to be just over ten minutes. It's taken us an hour, like we agreed."

While staring at Chan, Reyes said, "The EMP. They must have screwed with our timers again."

"Shit!" Chan said. "Um, *Crimson Destroyer*, we have a problem. There's only five minutes of oxygen left in the escape pod."

The operator on the *Crimson Destroyer* spoke in a sombre

tone. "I'm really sorry, but we *can't* get to you any sooner. We'll be there in ten minutes and twenty-two seconds."

The tablet shook in Chan's hand and she looked to be forcing her words out. "Okay. Thank you and see you then." She pressed a button to disconnect them. After the screen turned dark, she lifted her attention from the tablet to Reyes. "What the fuck are we going to do now?"

But Reyes' mind had gone elsewhere. The realisation tore her stomach out of her, and it took all she had to not vomit where she sat. "We had enough time to wait for my dad and Julius."

# CHAPTER 44

"Fuck!" Chan shouted while stamping on the floor. The loud snap of her boot against the black metal whipped through the small space. "What are we going to do? No one can hold their breath for five minutes. By the time the *Crimson Destroyer* gets here, we'll be dead."

"We had the time to wait for my dad and Julius," Reyes repeated.

Chan dropped down in front of Reyes and held her hands. Although she kept her tone level, the tension around her eyes and the tightness of her grip showed the truth of it. "I hate to say this, but we can't change that now. We have to work out how we're going to stay alive."

After letting her frame sag, Reyes looked back at Chan and nodded. Her dad would be furious with her if she didn't take positive action so close to being rescued. She stood up and walked over to the small computer in the wall. The warning next to the oxygen tank had dropped to four minutes and thirty seconds. "There must be a way. We're so close."

Before Reyes could say anything else, Chan grabbed her by the lapels. Although Reyes nearly swung for her, she saw something in the Marine's eyes that she hadn't seen before. Not rage like all of the other times. Confusion, pain, frustration, fear ... but not rage.

"I've always hated you," Chan said.

"What are you—?"

"Just shut up, Reyes, and let me talk for once. I saw what you had, and I hated you for that. I saw how lucky you were to have a dad that loved you like the WO did. He cherished you, no matter what. My experience of love is that it comes with conditions. If your dad had his own conditions, he kept them to himself. You were who you were, and he accepted that. Do you know what happened when I told my parents *I* was gay?"

"You're g—?"

"Come on, Reyes, are you that oblivious?"

Reyes stared at her small friend.

"They booked me in for therapy with a local religious zealot who claimed he could exorcise the devil from me. They didn't even have a god before then. But after that, they were all in, living their lives based on a book written by some man centuries ago. For the next two years, they quoted passages at me about how *wrong* I was. They ignored many parts in that cursed book if it didn't suit the life they wanted to live, but the very few vague lines about homosexuality became their mantra. Once, Mum even threw holy water at me and staged an intervention with my entire family."

Reyes felt Chan shake through the tight grip she had on her. She watched her eyes fill and glaze. "So why hate me?"

"Because you had it all. I know what you just said to your dad was a big deal. Believe me, I know that better than most. But I also knew he'd react how he just did. He already knew. We all did. For him, it didn't matter who you were. I could see he loved you no matter what. I've blamed you for that, and that's wrong."

Although Reyes opened her mouth to reply, Chan pushed a

finger across her lips to silence her. They stared at one another for several seconds before Chan leaned forwards.

After they'd kissed, Chan stepped back and rested against the escape pod's exit. Her eyes bloodshot, she watched Reyes for a moment before slamming a closed fist against the button on her right. A transparent screen shot across between them, cutting them off.

"What are you doing?" Reyes said.

For the next couple of seconds, Chan looked like she couldn't speak. She then drew a deep breath. "If I go, the oxygen release will slow down. It should give you eight or nine minutes. That'll be long enough."

Reyes banged against the glass shield separating them. "You haven't given me a choice. That's not fair. Why do *you* have to go? Why not me? Why not both of us?"

Crying harder than ever, Chan said, "Because you're *better* than me. I've known that about you from the second we met. The second I fell in love with you."

The air left Reyes' lungs, and although she opened and closed her mouth, she couldn't drag a response from her body.

"You have more to offer than I do. Besides, I couldn't live in a galaxy that you weren't in."

"Why didn't you say something sooner?"

"I've never been very good at expressing myself. Also, your secret was yours to tell, not mine to expose."

Choked with yet another wave of hot grief, Reyes shook her head at her friend.

Chan looked at the panel with the oxygen timer on it. It read four minutes. "I've got to go." Her fingers splayed when she pressed her palm to the window. "There's nothing you can do, Reyes. I've made this choice and not given you an option. Don't feel bad. I know you would switch places in a heartbeat, but you don't have that choice."

Mirroring Chan's action, Reyes raised a shaking hand to the other side of the cold glass.

"Make your dad and me proud. Do something great. Not that I need to tell you that, greatness is in your DNA." Chan then pressed the button to open the airlock.

As much as she looked like she tried to hide her suffering, Chan's eyes bulged, and convulsions snapped through her body. Suspended in the darkness of space, her tears froze and her mouth spread wide as if she tried to breathe the non-existent air. White frost covered her hair, and her lips turned blue.

It would have been easier to look away, but Reyes owed her more than that. A momentary glance at the oxygen timer on the wall, she saw it read seven minutes and forty-eight seconds.

CHAN HAD ADJUSTED THE TIMER ON THE TABLET AFTER THEY'D spoken to the *Crimson Destroyer*. Reyes still had a minute and a half before it arrived. She had just a few seconds of oxygen left. While watching the timer next to the oxygen tank count down, she drew a final deep breath—three … two … one—and held it.

As much as Reyes should watch the frozen corpse of a woman she'd never get to love, she had no oxygen left to breathe. Her grief nowhere near spent, she turned her back on her saviour and rubbed her stinging eyes. To watch Chan would force her to breathe. She needed to hold it together until the *Crimson Destroyer* arrived.

# CHAPTER 45

Reyes looked at her Shadow Order friends around her while wiping her eyes with the corner of her napkin. She laughed despite the weight in her heart and said, "I'm sorry."

They'd finished eating some time ago. Sparks had shoved their empty plates into the middle of the table because none of them had wanted to move away. The small Thrystian reached across and covered the back of Reyes' left hand with a gentle squeeze. Despite the pain of reliving what had happened on *The Faradis*, she looked across at Sparks and smiled, turning her hand over.

"Wait a minute," Seb said, his jaw loose. "You two?"

SA nudged him in the ribs before Bruke said, "Didn't you know?"

Seb shook his head. "No."

"You were the only one."

To see Seb's face flush made Reyes smile a little bit more. "It's okay. You've had to deal with your own feelings. With SA in front of you, it must have been hard to notice much beyond that."

His face even redder, Seb cleared his throat. "Well … um. Anyway, what are your plans now?"

"We're going back to Aloo. Sparks, Moses, and I are going to continue working for Pluto. They'll pay us a wage to have us on standby for when they need us."

Despite being the first one to hear her speak, Reyes still hadn't gotten used to the birdsong melody of SA's tone when she said, "Won't you stay a little longer?"

Maybe Moses saw Reyes was still reeling from the retelling of her story, because he spoke for them. "We need to get back to the Shadow Order's base for a briefing with Mr. H. He gave us the day off, but we promised we'd head back tonight."

With that, Reyes got to her feet, the others following suit. She walked over to SA and hugged her before moving on to Seb. He gripped her so tightly it almost hurt. In that one moment, he showed her more affection than he had for the entire time they'd known one another. When she pulled back, she smiled through her tears. "You're a good man, Seb Zodo." She looked at SA. "There's not many in this galaxy that do, but you deserve her. I hope you both enjoy your retirement."

Bruke stood at the end of the line. Just before Reyes could hug him, he said, "Can I come with you? I dunno, maybe do your admin or something. I've not got any fighting left in me, but I make a mean coffee."

The weight in Reyes' heart lifted as she took in the large creature. "Of course. I'd love you to."

Bruke smiled back and then turned to Seb. "You and SA deserve this time alone together."

As much as Seb looked like he might reply, he didn't. Instead, he nodded, stepped forward, and hugged his friend. When they separated, Seb was crying. To Reyes, he said, "You make sure you look after him, okay?"

Reyes nodded. "With my life."

The rest of the group said their goodbyes to one another before Moses led the way out of the dining room. Bruke and

Sparks followed next. Just before Reyes left, Seb grabbed her again and hugged her even tighter than before. He leaned close and whispered in her ear, "And please look after Sparks for me. I didn't want to say it in front of her, but I'll really miss her."

After they'd separated, Reyes smiled at Seb and SA. She'd said many goodbyes in her life. Many more than she'd like to. They were never easy. This time, she simply nodded at her two friends before turning her back on them and following the others from the room. She'd see them again. Of that she felt certain.

THE END.

Thank you for reading *The Faradis*, Book Eight of The Shadow Order, and the final book in the series.

*120 Seconds* is Reyes' story of her time on Q328. If you haven't read it yet, you can check it out at www.michaelrobertson.co.uk

**Support the Author**

Dear reader, as an independent author I don't have the resources of a huge publisher. If you like my work and would like to see more from me in the future, there are two things you can do to help: leaving a review, and a word-of-mouth referral.

Releasing a book takes many hours and hundreds of dollars. I love to write, and would love to continue to do so. All I ask is that you leave an Amazon review. It shows other readers that you've enjoyed the book and will encourage them to give it a try too. The review can be just one sentence, or as long as you like.

If you'd like to be notified of my news, discounts, and new releases, you can sign up to my spam-free mailing list at www.michaelrobertson.co.uk

**If you've enjoyed The Shadow Order, you may also enjoy my post-apocalyptic series - The Alpha Plague - Book 1**

**<u>The Alpha Plague - Available Now</u>**

MASKED - A PSYCHOLOGICAL HORROR

SOMETIMES IT'S BETTER TO NOT KNOW
WHAT'S UNDERNEATH ...

Jacob Davies is an alcoholic who's been sober for twenty years.
When he watches his dad lose his battle against pancreatic cancer it
sends his life into chaos and the cravings return stronger than ever.
Lost in his grief, he starts to see visions of a masked man that no one
else can see. A man who knows things Jacob is yet to find out. A man
who has answers to questions Jacob didn't realise he had.

Lucy, Jacob's wife, stood by him the first time he fell into alcoholism. As he starts to drink again, she makes it perfectly clear she won't do it a second time. Not now they have two teenage children to protect.

The visions and Jacob's grief send him on a journey that leads him to the brink of losing both his family and sanity. As he tries to hold everything together, maybe his only way out is to understand why he's seeing the masked figure ...

... Although maybe it will make everything a hell of a lot worse.

*Masked is a psychological horror about grief, addiction, and deceit.*

Masked is available to buy at www.michaelrobertson.co.uk

ABOUT THE AUTHOR

Like most children born in the seventies, Michael grew up with Star Wars in his life. An obsessive watcher of the films, and an avid reader from an early age, he found himself taken over with stories whenever he let his mind wander.

Those stories had to come out.

He hopes you enjoy reading his books as much as he does writing them.

Michael loves to travel when he can. He has a young family, who are his world, and when he's not reading, he enjoys walking so he can dream up more stories.

*Contact*
www.michaelrobertson.co.uk
subscribers@michaelrobertson.co.uk

~

Crash - A Dark Post-Apocalyptic Tale

Crash II: Highrise Hell

Crash III: There's No Place Like Home

Crash IV: Run Free

Crash V: The Final Showdown

~

New Reality: Truth

New Reality 2: Justice

New Reality 3: Fear

Made in the USA
Las Vegas, NV
17 July 2021